Ann Summers

True Passion: A Tale of Desire as Told to Madame B

Ann Summers

True Passion: A Tale of Desire
as Told to Madame B

EBURY
PRESS

1 3 5 7 9 10 8 6 4 2

Published in 2007 by Ebury Press, an imprint of Ebury Publishing

Ebury Publishing is a division of the Random House Group

Text written by Emily Dubberley © Ebury Press 2007

The Random House Group Limited Reg. No. 954009

Addresses for companies within the Random House Group can be found at
www.randomhouse.co.uk

A CIP catalogue record for this book is available from the British Library

The Random House Group Limited supports The Forest Stewardship
Council (FSC), the leading international forest certification organisation. All
our titles that are printed on Greenpeace approved FSC certified paper carry
the FSC logo. Our paper procurement policy can be found at
www.rbooks.co.uk/environment

Printed and bound in the UK by CPI Cox and Wyman, Reading, RG1 8EX

ISBN: 9780091924881

To buy books by your favourite authors and register for offers visit
www.rbooks.co.uk

FOREWORD

Welcome to Ann Summers' new collection of tales as confided to the mysterious Madame B. This is the first novella in this thrilling series, exploring the passions and dangers of an erotic relationship between a sexually adventurous young woman and her new lover.

I'm really excited to be able to bring you this tale of a woman who is bold enough to explore her deepest desires. We know that our customers are the sexually confident, fabulous women who love sex and aren't afraid to show it.

I promise that this exciting tale has something for each and every one of you. So, without any further ado, I will hand over to our hostess, Madame B ...

Jacqueline Gold

Dear Reader,

I am a collector of sexual confessions: true stories from women all around the world, women who have indulged their wildest sexual fantasies and passions to the full.

I thought that Katie's story was so intense and erotic that it deserved a book of its own. She has lived wildly and often shockingly, and has learned much from her many encounters.

I hope that you derive pleasure from the story of Katie and Alex, and that it might open some sexual doors for you that you haven't previously tried. It will certainly give you food for thought when you're in bed at night ...

Madame B x

CHAPTER ONE

Decadence

Katie switched her vibrator off and smiled at the man kneeling at the end of the bed, cock in hand – Tim? Tom? Something like that.

'It's good – but it's not as good as the real thing.'

She smiled to herself as he, predictably enough, ran his fingers up her thigh and into her wetness, simultaneously moving to plant his mouth on hers and kiss her in a way that let her know that she wasn't going to get any sleep for quite some time. Clearly he'd enjoyed the show she'd just put on for him. She let her body move against his, enjoying the feeling of his hard cock pressing against her thigh, manoeuvring herself skilfully away as he tried to slide his length against her slick pussy.

'I think you're forgetting something,' she said, reaching over to grab a condom, then ripping the packet open with her teeth. 'And anyway, there's plenty of time for that later.'

She put the condom on the pillow, still half encased in its foil, and slid down his body. As her lips touched his cock for the first time, he trembled, noticeably stiffening at her touch. She flickered her tongue around the tip, teasing him with deliberately light touches as she gripped the

3

base of his shaft and looked him straight in the eye. Then, still maintaining eye contact, she gradually sucked him deeper and deeper into her mouth until she could feel his glans pressing against the back of her throat, letting her tongue play over the sensitive underside at the same time.

'Fuck,' he moaned. 'Where did you learn that?'

She pulled away from his ever-thickening member, letting her breath play over it as she said, 'Do you really want me to tell you or do you just want me to carry on?' Sliding her lips back to the base of his cock in one slick move without waiting for an answer, she knew she'd made the right call when she tasted pre-cum at the back of her throat. As she felt the telltale pulses start, she pulled away.

'I want you to come on my face.'

He was more than willing to oblige. As he shuddered with what was obviously one hell of an orgasm, Katie ran her fingers through his cum and licked them clean.

'Fuck, you're a dirty bitch,' said the sated virtual stranger.

'You ain't seen nothing yet,' Katie said, and walked over to her toy chest, pondering exactly what to go for next.

❧

'So what happened with that bloke you left with last night?' asked Sophie. At 28 she was three years older than

Katie, but felt like a naïve kid when Katie described some of her adventures – she'd certainly got wilder over the five years they'd known each other.

'What do you think?' Katie said.

'Well, yes, it goes without saying that you had sex, but what was he like?'

'Bit vanilla for me, to be honest. Nice cock, though.'

'Vanilla?' Katie was always introducing Sophie to new words and phrases: BDSM, rimming, ATM. She was pretty sure that they weren't listed in any dictionary, but somehow Katie knew them all.

'Yeah, you know, straight. He was OK with coming on my face but when I tried to introduce him to strap on sex, he ran a mile. Wuss. It wasn't like he'd had any complaints about taking *me* up the arse.'

'You did only meet him yesterday.'

'Yeah, so he should have thought it was his lucky night. Most girls would have made him wait for anal, if they'd even let him get into their knickers in the first place, and if he wants to give it then he should be prepared to take it.'

'You're not most girls, though. Let's face it, you are, err, a bit wild.'

'I'm not *that* bad. I just don't see the point of holding out. You know how much shagging I missed out on when I was with Stuart. I'm just making up for lost time.'

Sophie tried not to let her doubts show on her face. She knew that Katie had been hurt by the split with Stuart: hardly surprising given they'd been together since she was 20. But they'd broken up over a year ago now, and Katie still wasn't showing any signs of calming down. At first, Sophie had thought Katie's experimentation was fine: apparently Stuart was a 'once a week at best' kind of guy and even she'd balk at that. She'd nursed Katie through the tears, reassuring her that she was attractive and sexy, that Stuart's lack of libido was about him not her. As Katie's confidence had improved and she'd told Sophie that she wanted to try all the things that she'd missed out on – along with a few she'd always fantasised about – it had seemed to make sense. Now, she wasn't so sure. Every weekend brought new stories of nights in fetish clubs or random group sex sessions. Even when Katie was 'safely' at home, she managed to pull. Sophie had to admit to being quite impressed by Katie's story about starting chatting to a cute celeb on Facebook and ending up having a phone sex session that night, which she'd followed up with the real thing two days later.

'Anyway, I enjoy it, so what's the problem? I'm being feminist: men have been allowed to shag around for years. Why shouldn't women?'

Katie's words broke into Sophie's thoughts.

'I guess. So, are you going to see him again? What was

his name anyway?'

'God, no. Can't remember his name and don't want to. I don't need another fuck-buddy. At least, not unless he can teach me something I don't know.'

Sophie rolled her eyes, knowing what was coming next.

'I mean, Ved's more than enough to keep me satisfied between men.'

Bloody Ved. Sophie didn't know what the appeal was but Katie seemed to adore the kinky bastard. OK, he was attractive: tall and toned, with a shaved head and big eyes that always had a mischievous twinkle about them. But some of the kinks he'd introduced Katie to made Sophie feel uncomfortable: paddles and crops, threesomes with guys and girls, snowballing – often with another guy's cum. She was as up for experimentation as the next girl but it all seemed a bit too 'porn' for her.

As if he had the table bugged – and Sophie wouldn't put it past him, listening in on a girlie conversation about sex could well fit into his warped fantasies – Katie's phone beeped with a text message.

'Speak of the devil,' she said, glancing at the screen. 'Ved's invited me to Decadence tonight. You want to come?'

'You know it's not my scene,' Sophie said. 'But thanks for the offer.'

'Your loss. Come on, let's go shopping. I've got nothing to wear.' Katie paused. 'Then again, that could work... But no.' She grinned. 'Ved decided to shave my pubes on Monday and now I'm all stubbly. What do you reckon? PVC, leather, or something really smutty?'

Sophie smiled. One thing she couldn't knock in Katie was her enthusiasm.

'I'm sure you'll find the perfect outfit. Guessing that H&M is out of the question?'

'I'll trade you – one boring shop for one fun one.'

'Deal.'

Sophie smiled wryly to herself. Maybe Ved and Katie were better matched than she thought. They certainly both had an unusual idea of 'fun'.

❧

By the time she got home, Katie was shattered. Shopping always took it out of her. She loved looking at her purchases laid out on her bed once she got home, and trying on her new clothes with old accessories, but all that squeezing through crowds of women in Primarni (as Sophie called it) and queuing for an age to try an outfit on in an all-too-often cramped changing room wasn't exactly top of her list of 'enjoyable ways to spend an afternoon'. At least the fetish shops tended to be emptier so there wasn't any of that hassle.

She wandered into the bathroom to run herself a bath. She'd treat herself with the full whammy: chilled cava, candles, an Anais Nin book and bathwater scented with a generous slug of her favourite sensual aromatherapy oil blend from the exclusive Treatment Rooms salon. In fact, she thought, 'Sod it,' and added bubble bath too. She needed some extra luxury after a hectic afternoon's shopping. Katie stripped off, and slipped into her fluffy green towelling bathrobe so she could go through to the kitchen and get her drink. She didn't want to give the neighbours a flash through the kitchen window: well, not unless the cute student who lived opposite was around.

When Katie finally sank into the water, she felt the waves of tension drifting from her body. Next to sex, baths were her favourite thing in the world. She lay back, self-indulgently enjoying the way her body looked at the various points it showed through the bath foam; a delicate curve of breast, her nipple just obscured by the foam; a slightly rounded feminine stomach and slim waist, flaring out at her jutting hip-bone; one long and elegant thigh raised out of the water for her to rest her book against. She was content with her body. Although she wasn't model-thin, she didn't need to do much exercise to maintain her slim lightly hourglass figure. Given the amount of compliments she'd had about her legs and arse – which had once elicited an actual gasp of excitement from a lover when he first saw it in the flesh – she had nothing to worry about there. When she was younger, she'd been paranoid about her small breasts but now she loved them: they were pert and she knew she'd never have to worry about them drooping. Her nipples were pink and highly sensitive, responding to the gentlest touch: when Ved got his nipple clamps and other toys involved, it was all she could do to hold back an orgasm from that alone.

Once the last bit of tension had escaped from Katie's shoulders, she threw the book onto the floor and started to buff her body all over, then reached for the razor to tidy up her stubble. Things were never dull at Decadence, and she wanted to be sure that she was prepared for every eventuality. Who knew what Ved would end up doing to her – and indeed, how many people would be watching at the time? The idea of being watched by a crowd of sexy strangers sent a delicious erotic shiver through Katie's body, and she knew that she'd be wet by the time she'd finished getting changed: anticipation was one of her ultimate aphrodisiacs and she enjoyed letting her mind turn over the myriad opportunities she might face. She was tempted to get her waterproof vibe from the bathroom cabinet but decided it'd be better to save herself for later. Her eyes glinted all the more enticingly when she was horny, and she didn't want to take the edge off her desire.

Getting out of the bath, Katie reached for her favourite 'Flirtigo' moisturising mist and sprayed it liberally over herself; rubbing it into her legs and arse, and lingering slightly longer than was strictly necessary over her breasts, making her nipples stiffen in response. She knew that the smell of the body spray drove Ved crazy, and she loved how soft it made her skin. Slipping her robe back on, she headed into her bedroom to get dressed.

It may have taken her three hours but Katie had to admit that the dress she'd finally found was absolutely perfect. Black leather with two white mod-style stripes down the front of it, the thing that had really sold it to her was the zip all the way down the front. That kind of detail could lead to so much fun. The dress fitted her so perfectly that it could have been designed specifically with her in mind, nipping in at the waist and clinging around her arse, only just skimming the bottom of her buttocks. She could bend over without showing her knickers but only because it was so tight. The soft suede lining felt great against her skin and she toyed with the idea of going commando, but decided against it. She was meeting Ved in town and didn't want to brave public transport in a dress quite this short without at least some protection. Anyway, Ved liked having her knickers stuffed in his mouth on occasion so she could always take them off at the club. She chose a simple silk thong, then pulled on a pair of knee-high sixties-style boots. The dress was too short to wear with stockings without the tops showing, and she didn't want to look like she was trying too hard. It also turned her on to think that, by merely undoing a zip, she'd be naked bar thong and boots. 'Almost forgot,' she thought, adding a black leather collar to the mix. Tonight she felt like being dominated and it was easy shorthand to indicate her desires.

With a slick of neutral lipstick, lashings of mascara and a quick spritz of shine spray over her hair, Katie was ready. Looking at herself in the mirror, she couldn't help but think how much she'd changed in the last year. She glanced at a picture on the bookshelf of her on a beach, back when she was still with Stuart. It showed a very different Katie: a stone heavier and wearing an unflattering swimsuit and sarong to cover herself up. It was obvious that she hadn't felt like a sexual woman. Her eyes gave her away the most. In the picture, they were flat, accepting that maybe life wasn't all that much to get excited about, and blandly reliable routine was the best you could hope for. Now, they sparkled. She didn't know what adventures the night would hold but she was certainly looking forward to finding out. She picked the photograph up and shoved it into a drawer on her way out the house.

Katie saw Ved the second she walked into Decadence. He wasn't hard to spot, in his slim-fitting military uniform, sitting in one of the four velvet-seated booths that were reserved for VIPs. Ved qualified by merit of seeming to know everyone: one week, he'd have the latest queen of the burlesque scene with him, the next a comedian with a top-rated TV show; sometimes it'd be a hot American porn star, others, an actress in the latest West End hit. No-one wanted to alienate Ved. He was too useful to know. Not that Katie liked him for his connections, though the limitless champagne that generally followed was a perk. She adored Ved because of his intelligence, his wit and his utterly deviant behaviour.

She'd met him at her first fetish night nearly a year ago, back when she was still nervous about what to expect. She'd hadn't even been wearing fetish gear – she cringed now, at the thought of making such a rookie mistake – and had only managed to get in because Ved had put his arm around her as he swept past her in the queue and said 'she's with me'. Once inside, he'd offered to show her around, and had watched with amusement as she'd taken in the sights with awe: a man on all fours wearing nothing but a thong and collar being led around on a lead by his Mistress; a woman tied to a six foot spider's web naked but for her stilettos; another woman screaming out as she was spanked by a man with a big leather paddle – and masturbating as he administered every 'thwack'.

'Scared, little girl?' Ved had asked her.

Although the words could have sounded creepy, from his lips, delivered with his deep and husky voice, they sounded intoxicating. She'd known at that moment that she had to have sex with him or she'd be regretting it forever after.

'It'd take more than that to scare me.'

'Brave words. I'll have to test them out later.'

Katie's pussy had flooded with juices at the mere thought and, sure enough, had been tested to her limits that night. Or so she'd thought. Somehow Ved had a way of introducing her to new limits every time they met, doing things she'd never even imagined people would do for fun back when she was Stuart's girlfriend. And she loved the way that her mind was expanding. She was pretty sure that she'd had more orgasms just from masturbating about her sessions with Ved than she'd had in the entire relationship with Stuart. Although it did make her blush to think about some of the things they'd done.

'Katie, babe.' Ved waved at her, beckoning her over. She walked deliberately slowly, giving him – and everyone else in the club – plenty of time to admire her new dress.

'Come, join us. This is Cat,' he said. A pretty blonde wearing a PVC nurse's uniform and stockings kissed Katie hello, aiming for her lips rather than her cheek. Katie was sure she felt a hint of tongue.

'Love your perfume,' Cat said. 'Come and sit next to me.' She moved her handbag to make room for Katie and patted the seat in invitation, placing her hand high up Katie's thigh and softly trailing her nails along the soft inner skin as soon as she sat down. 'Ved's told me so much about you. So what are you expecting here tonight?'

Katie was pretty sure that that was code for 'Ved's told me you do girls as well as guys – are you up for a three-some?' but didn't want to commit to anything so early in the evening.

'Who knows?' she said. 'I like to take things as they come.'

'And come again,' said Ved, drawing the attention back to himself again. 'Cat's a sweetie but she's such a filthy tart. I can't believe she got first grope of the evening with you in that delectable dress. I shall have to get double gropes later.' He gave Cat a playful flick of the crop he had in his lap. 'And you, my dear' – he arched an eyebrow at her – 'will get the punishment you deserve. Anyway, before Cat so rudely interrupted my introductions, I was about to say that this is Karl.' Dev gestured at a clearly gay but beautifully muscled 20-something to Katie's right, who looked vaguely familiar. 'And this is Emerald Glint.' Katie smiled at the voluptuous woman wearing a corset that was clearly ludicrously expensive, knowing from the name alone that she'd be one of Ved's burlesque 'friends'.

'Didn't I see your name on the bill for Velvet?' she asked.

'Oh, yes, I'm headlining there next week, doing an act with a rather naughty version of the Oscar statuette. Come along. Any friend of Ved's and all that.'

'Thanks,' Katie said, and was about to ask more about Emerald's act when she was interrupted first by Ved offering her a glass of champagne, and then by Cat's hand reappearing on her thigh and squeezing. Ved looked at it with mock disdain.

'Darling, please do put poor Katie down. She's barely got here. You'll be muff-diving her by the time she gets to her second drink at this rate.'

'Sounds good to me,' murmured Cat, shooting Katie a look that made her stomach flip with lust. OK, Cat was a little over-keen but she was utterly gorgeous. Katie was sure that Ved would love to see the contrast between her pale skin and dark hair, and Cat's golden tan and blonde locks, almost as much as she'd love seeing Cat stripped naked and begging to come. Added to which, Ved always gave her such delicious rewards when she gave him the sexual treat of watching her with another woman. Last time, she hadn't been able to walk properly for two days afterwards. She bit her lip to hold back the moan that threatened to escape her lips at the memory.

'So, sweetness, what have you been up to recently? Anyone good? Got any deliciously filthy anecdotes to share?'

Katie never ceased to be amazed by Ved's lack of jealousy. OK, she knew that he had sex with other women – sometimes in front of her – but she didn't want to know details of what he did when she wasn't around. She knew that Ved would be utterly unsuitable as a partner because of his party-boy lifestyle, but she didn't like to think of him coming as hard with another woman as he did with her. Even when they had group sex, she insisted that she was the only one that he actually fucked. He thought her ground rule was 'sweet' – though she suspected that was only because he had other women who were more than willing to play to whatever rules he set. He, on the other hand, relished every detail of her conquests: how big, how hard, how deviant. He'd even asked her about the taste of guy's cum before – albeit usually one that he was considering sucking off himself.

'Nothing special, darling. Hooked up with a random yesterday but he was a bit dull. I had to do all the work.'

'Should have Dommed him, petal. Put him through his paces.'

'It was hard enough convincing him to let me put a cock ring on him. He'd have run a mile if I'd got out a paddle.'

'Some people are just so boring. So, you're looking for fun tonight?'

'You know me, gorgeous.' Katie leaned over and gave Ved's cock a proprietory squeeze. 'I take it where I can get it.'

'Girls just want to have fun,' said Cat, putting her hand on top of the one Katie had on Ved's cock and squeezing her hand and his cock at once.

'Hmm, OK, definitely a bit too full-on,' Katie thought. 'But she's clearly up for playing.' She made a mental note to tell Ved that Cat would do for a three-way later if no-one better came along. But right now, she decided, as she took a sip of champagne, it was time to mingle. There was a particularly cute specimen in the corner who she hadn't seen before. If the size of the bulge in his tight black trousers was anything to go by, he was worthy of some exploration.

'Just going for a wander, back in a sec,' she said.

'I'll come with you,' Cat said.

'I've just seen someone I haven't hooked up with for a while and I want to catch up with them,' Katie lied. She wanted some time away from Cat to scout for other women, apart from anything else. Although Cat was stunning, the keenness was a bit of a turn-off. 'Sorry – but I won't be long.'

Cat pouted as Katie shimmied away, giving Ved a

subtle wink over her shoulder that she knew he'd understand as meaning 'Don't expect me back any time soon. I'll call you if anything fun's happening.'

Smiling seductively, Katie walked straight over to the fit stranger. 'Nice ... outfit,' she said, letting her eyes linger unashamedly over his cock as she looked him up and down.

'I could say the same,' the stranger replied, clearly appreciating Katie's form in her tiny dress. 'Easy access.'

'The dress is. I'm not,' Katie said, her flirtatious tone belying her words.

'Really? You like to make people wait?'

'I just don't see why something as much fun as sex has to be rushed. It's so much more tantalising if you're taken slowly to the edge then, just when you think you're going to topple, get pulled back and have to repeat the whole process again. I mean, the evening's barely begun. It's a bit early for *that*.' Katie gestured towards a couple fucking at the edge of the dance floor. 'They've hardly been here long enough to have decent foreplay.'

'If you like to take your time, let's talk. Follow me.'

Katie did as she was told, her eyes lingering on his pert butt as the stranger led her into the dungeon.

One of the perks of fetish clubs, thought Katie as she looked at the crowd around her, was that everything was so safe. There were marshals everywhere keeping a strict eye on proceedings, and a universal safe word to make it easy for them to know if and when to interject. All Katie had to do was say 'Red' and whatever indulgence she was suffering would stop. Right now, she was a long way from wanting to use the safe word. The stranger – she still hadn't asked his name, preferred the thrill of being dominated by an anonymous man – was fastening her wrists to a rack, stretching them tightly above her head so that she was powerless to move. He moved down to her ankles and bound them in a similar fashion, so that Katie was stretched wide open for all to see.

As soon as they'd got into the dungeon, having established her ground rules on the way there (no fucking, breathplay, bloodsports, extreme pain or watersports. Other than that, anything went, safe word allowing) he'd unzipped her dress and cruelly pinched her nipples. 'Strip,' he'd ordered, and she'd obliged, putting her dress into the black leather bag she'd brought with her just in case such a situation arose. She'd stood in front of him in her thong and boots.

'I said strip. That means everything.'

Katie felt a fizz of excitement in her clit at his masterful tone, and removed her boots and thong, now fully naked in front of at least 100 other people who were playing in the dungeon. Some openly stared at her and one guy commented, 'Nice tits,' but the majority just continued with what they were doing. Nonetheless, Katie felt vulnerable – in an incredibly sexy way. She could feel her juices bubbling up between her legs and knew that everyone in the room would be able to see her arousal unless she was very careful. When the stranger ordered her onto the rack, she realised that there was no way she'd be able to hide it. The thought of such a public humiliation turned her on.

Once Katie was fully secured, the guy looked at her exposed body properly for the first time, the growing bulge in his trousers showing that he liked what he saw.

'Comfortable?' he asked.

Katie nodded.

'Then I'll begin.'

He walked all the way around Katie on the rack, letting his eyes brazenly roam over her body.

'You do realise that I can do anything I want to you.'

Again, Katie nodded.

'Speak when you're spoken to. And only when you're spoken to,' the stranger said.

'Yes. You can do anything you want to me,' Katie said, feeling herself get wetter as she articulated the words.

'And you like that, don't you, you dirty little slut.' There was no question in his voice as he stared directly into her cunt. Katie was sure he'd be able to see her clit swelling, he was turning her on so much.

'I like it.'

'Good, good. So what shall I do with you? Maybe I'll start with a light whipping,' he said, picking up a rubber whip and trailing it over her body. Katie's gaze followed the trail of the fronds on her body. It felt soft as he pulled it lingeringly over her clavicle, around her breasts, over her nipples, down her stomach and oh-so-gradually over her open pussy.

'Look at that,' the guy said, pulling the whip away, still connected to Katie's pussy with a thin ribbon of her juices. 'You've got my whip wet with your juices. I don't work with dirty equipment. Lick it clean.' He pushed the whip into her mouth.

Katie did as she was told, not only feeling the humiliation of sucking her own juices off the rubber that filled her mouth to bursting, but also knowing that a wet whip stung so much more than a dry one. When he was satisfied it was 'clean' enough, the man pulled it from her mouth, and trailed it down her body once more, again puddling it in her juices. This time, he pressed harder, rubbing the whip against her clit and making her tremble. Then he pulled back to run just the very tips of the whip fronds over her clit, in a delicate tease that made Katie arch her hips up in an attempt to get more friction.

'Greedy girl. Plenty of time for that later,' the man said, pushing the whip into her mouth once more and removing the seductive pressure from her clit. As Katie sucked the whip clean, she thought how good her juices tasted. She could never understand why women got so hung up about men going down on them, worrying about the taste or smell. Pussy juice tasted lovely, whether hers or another woman's.

Clearly her lover agreed. After giving her two quick flicks of the whip, one to each nipple, making her eyes well up at the smarting sensation, he affixed nipple clamps to her reddening buds. He tightened them up, looking her in the eye as he did so, stopping just beyond Katie's comfort zone. Or so she'd thought beforehand – now she could feel herself getting wetter at the pain/pleasure mix that flooded her body.

The man affixed a long chain between the clamps, and checked it worked by giving it a quick tug. Katie winced at the pain, but felt her pussy contract in pleasure. Keeping the chain in his hand, the man moved between Katie's legs, and knelt to give the tip of her clit a long, soft lick. Katie moaned.

'I said you could only speak when spoken to. That includes moans. Be quiet,' the stranger said. 'Oh, and don't think I'm going to let you come. If you do, I'll leave you strapped here with your dripping pussy open for all to see for the rest of the night. I'll tighten these. And I'll come up with something even more fun to punish you with too.' He gave the chain another tug.

Katie's head rushed at the thought of what was happening: here she was, naked, exposed and with a man between her legs determined not to let her come despite going down on her in, if first impressions counted for anything, a scarily expert way. Part of her wanted to ignore his warnings just so she could find out what would happen if she allowed herself release. But, from the looks of the equipment in his bag, that would be one hell of a gamble. She closed her eyes and sank into the moment.

The man traced his tongue achingly slowly first up one of her lips, then the other. His delicacy made it all the more arousing. He repeated the stroke again, avoiding her clit and simply teasing. Katie could feel herself getting hornier by the second and pressed against her bonds, eager to push her pussy into his face, but unable to move more than a few millimetres. He kept this slow and steady progress up until she didn't think he'd ever lick her clit, then, in one fast move, he took her clit between his lips and softly sucked. Katie bit her lip to stop herself from moaning. A man in a rubber gladiator's outfit, who was watching her with obvious relish, met her eye and she knew he could tell how much the ministrations were working. She had to close her eyes in bliss when she felt her stranger's tongue flicker over her clit, pushing her clit hood back to expose the super-sensitive tip. Her clit felt three times its normal size as he expertly teased her, then pulled back to simply breathe over her.

'God, you get wet easily. You really are a filthy tramp.'

The humiliating words only added to her arousal as he returned to lap at her clit, this time sliding a finger inside her and expertly finding her G-spot at first thrust. He worried his finger against it, adding another when she gushed juices over him, and then opening his fingers to spread her wide. His tongue continued its relentless pace, slowly but with no hint that he was ever going to move from exactly where he was. Katie let herself drift off, feeling herself drawing ever nearer orgasm, when – 'Fuck!' – the man had yanked the chain, pulling her out of her reverie and eliciting the expletive from her lips.

'You spoke without being spoken to. Bad girl. No more pleasure for you,' the man said, moving from his position immediately.

He walked to her head and wiped his wet fingers over her face, before thrusting them into her mouth for her to lick clean. Once he was done, he pulled his cock out and stood next to Katie's head, masturbating directly over her mouth.

'You can see it and smell it, but if you try to touch it, you're in trouble,' he said. 'You clearly couldn't cope with me pleasuring you so I'm just going to have to use you for my own pleasure instead.'

Katie knew that her juices would be clearly visible

down her thighs by now. As if the humiliation wasn't enough, watching men wank always got her off, and this cock was a beauty: uncut – just the way she liked it – and although only slightly larger than average, it was perfectly shaped, with a thick base and lickable head. The vein that ran down his length was a temptation too – she wanted to run her tongue from root to top and back again, teasing him until he roughly thrust his cock into the back of her throat and made her swallow his load.

As he got nearer, she could smell his arousal and it took all her willpower not to lick her lips – he was so close to her face by now that even that act would bring her tongue into contact with his cock. She watched as he moved his hand up and down, making his cock grow ever-bigger, pre-cum making his head slick and shiny. Her clit was still throbbing from his expert cunnilingus and this view was only adding to her arousal. She began to worry that she might come merely from watching him and feeling the tight drag on her nipples from the clamps. By now, they were beginning to really smart, sending signals down to her clit with every pulse. This stranger really did know how to play her.

'By the way,' the man said, still stroking his cock, 'this is a friend. He'll be joining us.'

And still he kept upping the ante. Katie looked over to see that it was the gladiator who'd smiled at her earlier.

She knew that she only had to say the safe word to refuse the apparent order, but he was well muscled and wiry, with stunning blue eyes and a cheeky smile. Adding him to the equation was just a bonus. Anyway, she could do with some more attention. Maybe this guy would go down on her, given his friend was otherwise engaged?

Instead, he stood at the other side of Katie's face and pulled his cock out.

'Same rules,' said her Master. 'No touching him. We're just going to use you like a cheap whore and spatter our cum over your pretty face.'

Katie almost climaxed at his debauched words. When he handed the chain attached to the nipple clamps to his friend, who tugged it as he tugged his own – large, thick – member, she could feel herself start to shake.

'You said you like to wait,' her Master laughed. 'Well, I'll make you wait until you're begging me for release.'

He reached into his bag and placed a small remote-controlled vibrator on her clit, obviously enjoying seeing the look on her face as he started it buzzing: ecstasy at the sensation, and agony at being banned from coming.

'You're drawing quite a crowd too,' he said. 'Maybe I'll let them have a go with you once we've finished.'

Katie knew that would be beyond her limits but was pretty sure that his words were meant purely to turn her on. Then again, she hadn't ever met the guy before. Maybe he *did* mean it. The idea of being a sex toy for everyone in the club made her shudder in terrified anticipation: could her base desires override her sexual limits?

By now, both men were starting to groan.

'Open your mouth, slut,' the man ordered, 'and don't swallow. I want to see you with a nice mouthful of my spunk.'

'And mine,' his friend said. 'Take two loads at once, you dirty bitch.'

Katie opened her mouth wide and tried to resist the temptation to lick, but as the cum started spurting from the first guy, she couldn't resist lapping at the head, flickering her tongue between one cock and the other. That triggered the other man's orgasm and he shot more cum than she'd ever imagined it was possible to produce into her mouth, then pulled away to coat her cheeks, neck and tits.

The first guy recovered his breath after his orgasm then addressed Katie sternly.

'I told you no touching. Bad girl. You broke the rules. What *shall* we make your punishment?'

He turned the vibrator up another setting and pressed it hard against her clit. Katie could feel herself slipping over the edge into orgasm when he pulled it away. She gasped in frustration.

'I *was* going to let you come but I can't possibly reward

you for breaking the rules. Still, you are quite sweet so I'll give you a choice. I'll untie you now and you can go back to your friends, though you're not allowed to clean your face so they *will* see what a slut you've been. Or I'll give you an orgasm here – but you'll have to stay here tied up and spread open for half an hour first, with everyone staring at you. I'm thirsty. I want to go to the bar and I can't be bothered to make you come before I do.'

Much as Katie was scared of being left tied up, and desperate to come, she wanted to climax at this man's hands – and tongue. He was too expert to miss out on.

'Make me come,' she said.

'Say please.'

'Please make me come.'

'OK, back soon. Enjoy. No coming before I get back.'

And putting the vibrator back on her clit, on a setting that was dangerously likely to trigger her orgasm, he meticulously wrote something across her torso and wandered off. It took a while for Katie to work out that it said 'Booked until 9pm, do not touch. For reservations call this number' with a mobile underneath it. He was making her look like a whore – and she loved it. Holding back her orgasm for the next half hour was going to be hell.

❧

Half an hour later, every inch of Katie's body was trembling with the effort of holding her orgasm back. She was biting her lip as the toy buzzed away on her clit, somehow seeming to move up and down while it vibrated over her most sensitive parts. She closed her eyes, trying not to look at any of the people who were watching her trial, some openly masturbating, for fear that she'd see something that would tip her over the edge. She'd felt totally humiliated being spread open for all to see, and nervous that the guy might not come back at all, leaving her in her vulnerable state for the rest of the night.

Luckily – or perhaps not – everyone paid attention to the sign, and although she'd noticed a few people writing down the number, no one had touched her, in part thanks to a marshal who'd never seemed to stray far from her side. She wondered what would happen if the marshal moved away. Although the rules were strict, she was in a somewhat compromising position and there'd certainly be time for someone to slide a finger, tongue, toy or cock inside her before she could say the safe word.

She realised that, really, all of the men or women in the dungeon potentially had her at their mercy – and she'd already seen some serious players around tonight, who would probably try to push her further than she'd ever gone before. She bit her lip again. She had to stop thinking about it. The idea was too enticing and if she lost her focus she'd come. She considered lying to the stranger if she did, but somehow, she knew, he'd know. And if her punishment for licking his cock was half an hour of being displayed like a whore, who knew what he'd do to her if she dared to come? Again, she tried to shift her thoughts onto anything but sex, in the hope of fending off her orgasm, but the toy and nipple clamps made it hard for her to think about anything else, even if she closed her eyes to block out the sexy view.

When the stranger finally returned and slipped a wedge of banknotes into the marshal's hand, Katie realised why she'd been so carefully looked over. He'd paid the marshal off. Even though she'd felt exposed, she'd actually been entirely safe throughout. He'd played her again; making her feel scared of what might happen to heighten her arousal. When she looked at him, clearly projecting the word 'bastard' at him, if not actually saying it, he grinned.

'Enjoy yourself, dearie?' he said.

'Fuck, yes, you evil sod,' she said, body squirming as the stranger trailed a lazy finger from her lips to her pussy.

'Want that orgasm now, do you?'

'Please.'

'Shall I shove my cock inside you and make you come around it then?'

Swine! He knew that was one thing she wouldn't do.

Katie was more tempted than she'd ever been before but decided to stick to her ground rules. She never liked her first actual fuck with a new man to be in public: preferred to keep those first moments when cock meets cunt for herself. You could never tell how well a cock would fit until you tried it, after all, and she didn't want to have to go through the motions of bad first-time sex with other people watching. Conversely, she didn't want to share great first-time sex with observers: there was an intimacy to it that she liked to savour on her own. Ved, of course, called her a prude but she liked having at least some limits that she wouldn't break.

'No,' she said, terrified that he'd deny her orgasm as revenge for her chastity.

'Gosh, you really do stick to your principles, don't you?' the man said. 'Ah well, I guess a promise is a promise. But you've still got to wait until I tell you to come.'

He knelt between her legs and rubbed his fingers through her slick wetness, groaning in quiet appreciation. Then, without warning, he sucked Katie's clit into his mouth, at the same time pressing the vibrator against her pubic bone and sliding two fingers inside her. She tensed every muscle in her body to hold her orgasm back.

'Christ, you're wet,' he said, and slid another finger inside her, making her moan with delight.

'So you like being filled. Want more?'

Katie was almost delirious with pleasure. 'Fuck, yes. Fill me up,' she said.

'As you wish,' said the stranger and, with a few nifty twists and a squirt of lube, his fist was buried inside her.

'God, that was easy,' he said. 'You really are outrageously turned on. Anyone would think that you like being treated as a dirty slut.' As he spoke, he punctuated his words by pushing his hand ever deeper inside her.

Now, Katie was squirming around on his hand, body stretched to the limit, nipples on fire from the cruel clamps that still gripped her tightly. She wasn't sure that she could take much more, so intense was the feeling of his fist pressing against her G-spot, her skin stretched tightly down to pull her clitoral hood tightly against her (by now throbbing) clit.

'Open your eyes,' the man said, and Katie did as she was told, only to see Cat and Ved looking on in amusement from only inches away, Ved's hand buried in Cat's knickers. The stranger had clearly seen her with them earlier and invited them along to enjoy the show.

'Nothing like the company of friends to spice things up, I always find,' he said. 'Imagine how you must look to them, dripping wet, sweating, stretched wide and with a total stranger's hand buried in your cunt. They must think you're such a whore. Bet you they tell everyone you know about what they've seen.'

He'd done it again: added a further layer of public humiliation to the mix. Katie started breathing deeply to stop herself from coming. She knew she couldn't hold back for much longer.

As it was, she didn't have to. Katie was alternating glances between Ved, Cat and the sight of the stranger's hand buried inside her. She wished that she could reach down to grab his wrist and feel how far inside her he'd managed to get. She knew that it was way beyond the knuckles: and she was certainly glad that he wasn't wearing a watch. The idea of having this man's whole hand inside her was mentally arousing, as well as being so physically intense that her orgasm was beginning to build from the very depths of her cunt.

Cat mouthed 'I want you' just as the stranger sharply pulled the clamps from her nipples, sending pain flooding through her body as the blood rushed back into them. He pushed his fist inside her, deep, hard and fast, and ordered her 'Come', dropping his mouth to her clit and flickering his tongue over her as soon as he'd spoken. The release was instant: he'd taken her into the zone to such a degree that her body was his to control. As Katie came in the longest, loudest, hardest orgasm she'd had in a long time, the stranger kept his lips locked around her clit, softly sucking every last pulse of orgasm he could get from her trembling body. When the feelings finally managed to ebb away from her, the stranger kissed her on the cheek.

'Want me to untie you now?'

Katie was beginning to ache from being in the same position for so long, and nodded, thanking the stranger for his time.

'Any time, darling. Here's my number. Give me a call some time. After all, you'll probably have some messages to listen to from people who wanted to make an appointment with you. Maybe we can invite some of them round to join us?'

This was the kind of guy Katie wanted for a fuck-buddy: one who could play her and push her, tease her and finally satisfy her. Hell, his cunnilingus was so good that even if he'd only been a quarter of kinky, she'd have willingly seen him again.

'No probs… ' She glanced at his card. 'Joe. Pleasure meeting you. My name's Katie.'

'Oh, I know,' he said. 'I've been wanting to corrupt you for quite some time. Have fun.' And with that, he left. Katie joined Ved and Cat, endorphins buzzing through her body, giving her a natural high.

Katie's display had done nothing to dull Cat's enthusiasm. 'Shame he untied you,' she said. 'I was quite enjoying the sight of you tied up and at my mercy like that.'

'Maybe later,' said Katie. 'Right now, I need a drink.'

After such an intense power game, she needed a break before she got into another scene – although the idea of a gentle Sapphic session was a lot more appealing now than it had been earlier. Having a soft tongue and stubble-free face pushed into her aching cunt could be just what she needed to recover, Katie thought. She wondered if Ved would mind if she borrowed Cat for some girl-on-girl action – she wasn't sure she had the energy for a three-way now. She guessed he'd be fine, as long as he could watch. Linking her arm in Cat's, she leaned in close and whispered ' ...and if you're really good, maybe *I'll* be the one tying *you* up.'

It was just another normal night at Decadence.

CHAPTER TWO

First Encounter

Katie half-opened her eyes and reached blearily for her alarm clock, which was insistently bleeping at her to wake up. Hitting the snooze button, she settled back for that extra five minutes' sleep that always seemed so much more precious because it was time-limited. She was determined not to do her usual trick of hitting the snooze button repeatedly and starting her day late. It had been a long night – actually, a long weekend – but she had a lot that she needed to get sorted. Although the marketing agency she worked for had a flexitime policy, she had meetings all afternoon and had agreed to catch up with Sophie over drinks at seven so wouldn't be able to work late. There was no way she was going to clear her in-tray unless she left for work soon.

Katie regretted agreeing to see Sophie. Even though she loved her company, and hadn't had a chance to fill her in on all the details about Decadence because she'd been 'otherwise engaged', she could really do with a quiet night in. Cat had been more voracious than she'd expected, and she'd lost track of the amount of wine they'd had to drink over the last day or so while they were playing. Ved had been no help, encouraging them to try ever wilder things, until he got a call from another fuck-buddy inviting him to an impromptu orgy, and left them to enjoy some time alone. She'd managed to avoid a hangover by downing several pints of water once Cat finally left on Sunday evening, but she could still feel a dull ache in her pussy that reminded her of the weekend's excesses. She was tempted to give herself a quick orgasm at the memories that flashed into her mind, but knew that would just send her to sleep again. Morning masturbation was always a risk. And so, when the alarm went off again, Katie dragged herself from bed and went to the kitchen to make a stiff coffee. Leaving the premium Columbian Roast steeping in the cafetiere, she headed straight for the shower, hoping that her Original Source Mint shampoo would do its usual trick of perking her up.

Fifteen minutes later, Katie was beginning to feel at least primate, if not fully human. She picked out her favourite Karen Millen suit, and teamed it with a silk vest top. Adding sheer hold ups and a subtle silver pendant – a present from Stuart that still gave her a pang of nostalgia to wear but was so elegant that she was prepared to ride the feeling out – she was content with her outfit. It was the perfect combination of sexy and businesslike: going commando always gave her an extra frisson. Braving the mirror, she was pleased to note that the weekend's ravages didn't show on her face too obviously – though if anyone saw the shag bruises on her thighs, they'd definitely have questions to ask. In fact… She slipped off her jacket to check her upper arms for tell-tale thumb-grip bruises. She was in the clear – no need for concealer there. She applied a light layer of Clarin's Beauty Flash Balm, put a couple of sweeps of concealer over the slightly dark circles under her eyes, powdered her face then added her favourite lash-lengthening mascara and 'work bitch' red lippy. She smiled at her reflection: perfect. She was ready for the day ahead.

By noon, Katie was feeling less content. The phone had been ringing constantly with – mostly foolish – demands from clients and journalists. Could she change the creative for the ad campaign? The boss's wife thought it needed to be a bit pinker. (No, it went to press last week after three months of approvals and sign-off meetings, as you well know.) Could she arrange for four more tickets to the champagne launch on Friday to be biked over? (No, I know that you're probably not even going to write about the product and you're only asking because you want to bring your ligging mates along.) Could she call in some champagne glasses to go into the goodie bags for Friday? (Only if you don't want them to fit in the goodie bags – I deliberately got small bags because you told me they only needed to hold vouchers and a couple of coasters, and they were £1 cheaper than the larger ones.) At least her meetings would give her a chance to get out of the office and away from the phone. As she left the building, she switched her mobile phone off. 'Fuck it, I can always pretend the client turned up early for lunch,' she thought.

Things got no better as the afternoon progressed. Her first client turned up 25 minutes late, then complained that they hadn't had enough time together when Katie had to make her excuses in order to get to her next meeting on time, and had to skip her beloved espresso at the end of the meal. Nonetheless, in her efforts to appease the first client, Katie ended up making herself late for the second client, which she was sure would get reported back to her boss, Gemma, because client number two was renowned for moaning about the tiniest thing going wrong, and there were rumours that he had quite a 'close' relationship with Gemma.

As to the third client – 'Bah!', Katie felt her hands forming fists as she thought of him. Although he was only in his thirties, he seemed to have a 1950s view of women. He'd opened by asking her where 'the boss I saw last time' was because he 'didn't want to talk to a junior'. Katie patiently explained that she was a senior marketing manager, and was actually superior to the account manager who he'd seen before (she'd given him a chance, thinking he'd be able to handle a meeting on his own, but he hadn't come back with enough information for them to put together a proper pitch so she'd had to step in). As she spoke, she could tell that the client didn't believe her. More to the point, he seemed unable to look her in the eye, instead choosing to talk to her breasts. Katie was tempted to nip into the loo and draw eyes around her nipples, then come back in topless, but was pretty sure that wouldn't be helpful. More to the point, she could think of few men she fancied less, and didn't want to give him the privilege of seeing her in a state of undress.

When her meeting with the sexist from hell finally finished and Katie turned her phone back on, it immediately lit up with a message saying 'You have three missed calls', and, when she killed that, 'You have four new text messages.' She listened to the voicemails, relieved that there was only one 'crisis' to deal with and even that could wait until morning because the journalist she needed to speak to would have gone home already. Flicking through the text messages, she discarded one from an unknown number, thanking her for a great night. It was signed 'Tom'. 'So that was what Friday night's bloke was called,' Katie thought. She skimmed through the one from her mum, asking her to call for a catch-up when she got a chance, and deleted another message from her phone network offering 'bargain calls and a free upgrade'.

'Whoopy-fucking-do,' she thought.

When she saw the name 'Sophie' on her last message, she assumed the worst. 'Bloody hell, she's not going to cancel on me, is she? That'd be the cherry on top of an all-round shitty day.' Even though Katie was tired, the thought of offloading to Sophie about her last client of the day had been the only thing that had pulled her through without punching him. But no, not quite. 'Still on for 7 at Red Bar? Really sorry but I've got a mate of my brother's in tow – forgot he was in town and I'd said I'd put him up.' Feeling tetchy, Katie headed for the bus into town. The last thing she needed to do right now was make small talk with a stranger. Still, maybe he'd go away if she kept the conversation smutty enough: it was always a good way to embarrass men. She hurriedly texted Sophie back. 'Might be ten mins or so late due to client from hell but be there soon. Looking forward to it x.'

Katie couldn't see Sophie when she walked into the Red Bar. Just to pour salt into the wound of her lousy day, it was packed with people and all the tables were taken. She and Sophie deliberately met at Red because it was minutes away from Sophie's studio so she could usually turn up early before the office crowd nabbed all the tables. 'One of the joys of working for yourself,' she'd said to Katie. 'You can clock off whenever you want.' But today Sophie had clearly got stuck at work too, so they'd have to stand. 'Bloody great,' Katie thought. A hubbub of 'Rah rah rah' conversation filled the air and she had to take a few deep breaths before she could bring herself to squeeze through the throng to the bar and order her favourite Polish Prince cocktail.

The first sip was like nectar: an appley sweetness teamed with the sharpness of lime juice. Katie felt her sanity restoring as she took a heftier swig, and the alcohol flamed her throat. She grabbed a bar stool from underneath a chinless wonder's coat, giving him a quick nod of thanks before he could protest, and sat down on it, managing to position her elbows so that no one got too close. She looked at her mobile phone: 7.20 and no message from Sophie to say that she was running late. She was usually so good about things like that. Hmm. Maybe she'd been there all along and Katie had missed her?

Katie glanced around the bar again: one table full of women who were clearly either WAGS or promo girls – the orange tans and sparkling white teeth were a dead give-away; another with a couple whose ludicrously self-indulgent public displays of affection were attracting jibes from the table full of obvious sales boys next to them; and in the corner, a guy sitting on his own, with two drinks in front of him. 'Mmmm, cute,' Katie thought, taking in his sandy hair, smiling eyes and slim but muscular build. She was just considering going over to introduce herself – and possibly face the wrath of an irate girlfriend – when she saw Sophie walking up the stairs that led from the toilets, and heading straight for the table. 'Must be her brother's mate,' Katie thought, realising that that probably placed him in his mid-thirties. 'A bit old for me, but then again, with age comes experience.' Maybe he wasn't going to be such a drain on her evening after all. Of course, she'd have to check that Sophie wasn't interested first: they had a deal that she'd never go after any guy that Sophie fancied. But given that Sophie tended to prefer dark and swarthy men with builder's bodies, and was a curvy redhead with pre-Raphaelite curls tumbling down her back so tended to attract a different kind of man to Katie, she didn't think it would be a problem.

Katie ordered a round of drinks – another Polish Prince for her, Sophie's favourite Cosmopolitan (she didn't care that it had gone out of fashion. She liked the taste) and a bottle of the beer that she could see on the table in front of the mystery man. OK, he might not want another one but at least she'd get points for making an effort: politeness cost nothing (or at least, only £3.50). After asking for a tray from the barman to avoid the embarrassment of struggling through a crowded bar carrying three drinks, she ran her fingers through her hair to fluff it up, applied a coat of lip gloss using the silver change tray as a surrogate mirror, then picked up the drinks. She reached the table without incident and with a cry of, 'Babe, didn't see you here – I've been at the bar. Got us a round in,' she joined her best mate and the delectable stranger.

Ten minutes later, Katie had learned that the stranger was called Alex, he'd gone to school with Sophie's brother Mark which would make him about 34 if her memory served, and he was in the process of moving to London for work but needed somewhere to crash while he sorted out a flat.

'So Sophie kindly offered to help out?' Katie asked, wondering why Alex wasn't staying with Mark – after all, they were the friends.

'Well, Mark's right on the outskirts of London and Alex is looking for somewhere central so it made a lot more sense if he stayed with me,' Sophie said.

'She's an angel – and what a stunning flat. I can't believe how big the windows are – and that view. It's a long way from that treehouse I helped you make, eh?' He ruffled Sophie's hair.

'So you've known Sophie since she was a kid?' OK, Katie guessed it made sense if Alex had been to school with Mark but she couldn't help but be curious. She'd never heard Sophie mention an Alex before, and she'd quizzed her often enough about eligible blokes she knew. Surely she'd have realised that Alex was exactly the kind of man Katie went for?

'Soph's like a little sister to me. I missed you when I was in New York,' Alex said, diverting his attention to Sophie. 'Eight years is a long time.'

'Too long, Alex. But it's great to have you back.' Sophie reached over to squeeze Alex's hand.

'I bet Sophie's grown up a lot since you last saw her,' Katie said, trying to establish the relationship between the two of them without being too obvious. They seemed pretty touchy-feely.

'Well, obviously she's not an annoying teenager any more,' Alex said. 'But she's always going to be "little sister Soph" to me.'

'Thank God for that,' Sophie said, knowing Katie well enough to see what she was digging for. 'Not being funny but, err, anything else would be weird. I mean, even though you've picked up a bit of an accent you're – well – you're still Alex. Or should that be Zitty?'

'God, don't remind me,' said Alex, taking the dig in the good-natured way it was intended. 'I thought my acne would never go away. Then I hit 25 and it went overnight.'

'Being a spotty teenager is a sign of high testosterone, you know?' Katie said. 'It suggests you'll be a fantastic lover in later life.' Now that she knew Sophie wasn't interested, her way was clear to flirt.

Alex blushed. 'Really? Well, I'm not sure about that. But it's certainly a lot easier to pull when you haven't got a face that looks like a pizza.'

'I'm sure it is,' Katie purred, then clocked Sophie's 'Oi, this is supposed to be *our* night, stop trying to pull my mate,' look.

'So anyway, Soph. What's been going on with you, other than having a fit mate land on your doorstep?' Well, there was no harm in letting him know that she thought he was attractive, was there? But as Sophie started to describe the latest design project she'd landed, Katie gave her her full attention. 'Mates before meat' was one of her personal rules. Even when there was someone as tempting as Alex around.

Nonetheless, as soon as Alex went to the loo, Katie started to quiz Sophie.

'So what's he like? Worth playing with?'

'Can't you think about anything else?' Sophie said. 'He's practically a brother to me. I don't see him that way. Anyway, I haven't seen him for an age and we drifted out of email contact about five years ago.'

'You must at least know whether he's single?'

Sophie sighed. 'OK, yes. He did mention that it was good to be back and away from all the hassles of New York. I got the impression that there might have been a woman involved although I haven't had a chance to get any details. We had only been here for half an hour when you turned up.'

'Fair enough. But he's staying with you for – how long?'

'Depends how long it takes him to get a flat but it's probably going to be at least a week. Could even be a month. You know what it's like finding somewhere decent. And it's not as if I don't have the space.'

Sophie had found a silver lining when her favourite great aunt had died, in the form of a three-floor central London artist's studio that no one in the family had even realised existed, and had been the subject of salacious gossip ever since. Sophie had spent hours with Aunt Kittie talking about painting when she was a child, and had gone to St Martins as a direct result of those conversations. Her great aunt had apparently been considered to have 'quite some talent' in art in her youth, but had given it up when she met the man who was to become her husband and fell pregnant within a month of marriage. It just wasn't the done thing to have a career in those days, and it was only when Kittie's daughter Daisy was old enough to leave home that she'd started painting again, refusing to show the pictures to anyone but her closest family members. Sophie was always the first, particularly after Daisy had upped sticks and gone to India, leaving no explanation of why she'd left and breaking her mother's heart. From that day forward, Kittie had closed off to everyone except Sophie, throwing herself into her painting as emotional release. Sophie had felt a particular flush of happiness when she took Kittie to her degree show and saw the pride in her eyes – even more so than when she later got her results through and found out she'd got a first. But art is no way to make a living in the real world and Sophie had been about to give up on it despite getting a few good reviews in some of the smaller art magazines, when Aunt Kittie had had a fall, broken her hip and gone into rapid decline. Sophie had been inconsolable for weeks after she died. Then the letter had come through giving Sophie the deeds to the building: there was no explanation as to how Aunt Kittie had come to own it, but the lawyers insisted it was all legitimate. After that, it seemed churlish to give up, particularly given that Aunt Kittie had stated in her will that it was to help Sophie follow her dreams. She rented out the downstairs apartment to cover her living costs, and lived and worked on the top two floors.

'Well even if he's only with you for a week it gives you plenty of time to get up to speed and tell your best mate all about it, doesn't it?' Katie said.

Sophie smiled. 'The things I do for you. OK, fine, I'll do it, as long as you promise to behave for the rest of the night and just be "normal Katie" instead of "nympho

Katie". But don't break him. He's a lovely bloke and I don't want him getting hurt.'

'Fine, fine. As if I'd hurt him. Well, not unless he asked me to. Anyway, what man doesn't want easy sex when they've just arrived in a strange town? I'd be doing a public service.'

But before Sophie could answer, Alex had returned, putting a stop to the conversation.

By 10pm, Katie was on her fourth cocktail and beginning to feel slightly tipsy. True to her word, she'd backed off from Alex, instead letting Sophie lead the conversation. Katie loved it when Sophie took centre stage. She was a great conversationalist but she was usually too shy to let go unless it was just her and Katie; in a group she tended to let other people dominate, preferring to express herself publicly through her art. But Sophie was clearly at ease with Alex. More to the point, she was excited about her new commission – a giant canvas of an A-lister's girlfriend, which he wanted to surprise her with on her 30th birthday. In typical Sophie manner, she'd spent half an hour explaining the new technique she was going to test out for her latest client, which could have been boring had it come from anyone else, but in her case kept both Alex and Katie gripped, because her passion was so intense and they both loved her. Only then did Sophie finally mention who it was for, at which point both her listeners went slack-jawed with awe. The star was so big that it was impossible not to have heard of him.

'Not being funny but how the hell did you land that?' Katie asked. 'I mean, you're obviously brilliant but he's massive. I didn't even know he was in the UK.'

'He's filming over here and he saw a picture I'd got up in Carlotta's.'

'The little coffee shop at the end of your road?'

'That's the place. Apparently he's a fan of good coffee and someone had told him it was the best place to go. So there he was, getting his espresso, and he saw one of my Naïve-inspired pictures. He scribbled down the number on the bottom of the painting and the rest is history.'

'So you answered the phone and you'd got him on the end of it?'

'God, no. I thought I'd be dealing with his PA – she was the one who'd called to find out how much I'd charge and make the appointment. When she told me who it was for, I thought it was a wind-up at first, but I checked her name on Google and sure enough, she came up as his PA. I figured that she'd just bring along the girlfriend – Celia Chah, you heard of her? – for a sitting and that would be it – I mean, he's a busy man. Have you seen how many films he's in this summer? So when I opened the door at ten and he was there in the flesh, I had to focus on not staring at him. I thought I was still asleep and dreaming.'

'What was he like?' From his tone of voice it was obvious that even Alex was a bit star-struck at the mention of this particular celeb – he was as much of a man's man as a woman's wet dream.

'Was he as gorgeous in real life as he is in the flesh?' Katie didn't really fancy the star but it was an obvious question. Although she could see his appeal, he was a bit plastic for her but there was no harm in making Alex realise that other men could catch her eye.

'He was utterly charming, a real gent. If I hadn't seen all his films, there's no way that I'd have been able to tell that he was famous from his attitude. He was really polite.'

'Yeah, because politeness is just what we all want in a man,' said Katie.

'Oh come on, you don't want some Neanderthal who's just going to grunt at you,' said Sophie.

'I dunno. The guy I was with at Decadence on Saturday didn't do a lot more than grunt, and that was fine by me. In fact a lot more than fine.'

'What's Decadence?' asked Alex.

'I'll take you some time,' said Katie. 'You'll love it.' She lowered her voice, and leant closely into Alex's body so that she could murmur in his ear, 'Anything goes there. And I mean anything. Couples openly fucking – lesbian, gay and straight alike – leather, rubber, people getting spanked in the dungeon. I even saw a naked firebreathing dwarf there once. I'll get a group together – we can all go to celebrate you moving back to London.'

'Err, thanks for the offer but it's not really my kind of place,' said Alex, leaning back to reclaim his personal space.

'Don't be daft, there's nothing to worry about. You'd have a great time. It's three floors of fantastic music, sexy people and limitless opportunities. What's not to like? I'm sure we can dig out an outfit for you from somewhere if you can't find one. Even Sophie came to my birthday party there last year and she had fun, didn't you, babe?'

Sophie made a non-committal noise that didn't clearly imply which side of the argument she was on.

'See, everyone loves it. Live a little.'

'No, I told you, I don't like all that kind of thing. It's just not me, all that pseudo-sexy "isn't perversion great" stuff.' Alex was flushing as he got more insistent. 'If you ask me, most of the people there are just faking it to be fashionable.'

'Oh, I can promise you there was no faking it on Saturday night. You're just scared because it's something new. Typical uptight Yank. I thought you were a real man,' Katie said, riled by his attitude towards 'her' club. 'Open your mind.'

'I'm not a Yank and my mind's perfectly open, thanks very much.' By now, Alex's voice was becoming clipped.

'So anyway, Soph, does this commission mean you're going to be hanging out with A-listers all the time now?'

Alex turned his body slightly away from Katie, in a subtle but obvious snub.

'I wish!' Sophie said, who'd been occupied by trying to find her purse so had missed the tail end of the exchange. 'But no, he just dropped over some pictures for me to base the painting on. His girlfriend can't come to a sitting, for obvious reasons if you think about it. I mean, it'd hardly be a very good secret present if she did, would it?'

'True. So how long have you got to do it?' said Alex.

'That's the one thing that I'm worried about. I've only got a month. I want it to be as good as I can make it but it'd be hard enough to get it perfect in that time if she was doing multiple sittings, let alone just from pics. How am I going to be able to get an idea of her personality from a load of still images? Still, I wasn't going to say no to an opportunity like that now, was I? Hell, a girl can try.'

'A girl can succeed,' Katie said vehemently. 'Particularly when she's as talented as you are. I'll get one of the PR bunnies at work to start collecting any clippings they see on her when they're doing their usual trawl of the papers for me if you want?'

'That's so sweet. OK, she probably won't show inner soul to the paps but at least it'll give me something to go on. He's only been dating her for a month and you know

I'm not exactly a fan of *Heat* so I don't know the first thing about her. Thanks, babe. You're a star,' said Sophie.

'Well, just think, if this one goes well, you could end up doing pics for all the celebs,' joked Katie, trying to play down the gesture. 'Maybe you should give David Tennant's agent a call, offer him cheap rates?'

'And you wouldn't have any vested interest in that at all, then, would you?' Sophie joked, knowing about Katie's crush on the svelte star in all too much detail.

'Oh, go on, what are friends for?' She paused for a second then added, 'I bet *he'd* come to Decadence,' under her breath, pointedly looking at Alex as she spoke.

He ignored her in an equally pointed way.

The impasse didn't last long – the pair were eager to let Sophie enjoy her moment of glory and kept asking her about the star, even though she swore, 'There's not much to tell. He was only at the studio for half an hour.' Time flew and before long, the bar was calling last orders.

'One more for the road?' asked Sophie.

'I'd better not,' Katie said. 'Work in the morning and I've got to get back.'

Although she loved Sophie, she was worried that if she had another drink she might get back onto the subject of Decadence with Alex, and she didn't want to ruin the night. How dare he call her and her mates perverts? He was just an uptight wanker who clearly didn't know what he was on about.

'You can stay at mine if you want,' Sophie said. 'You know you're always welcome to borrow my clothes.'

'Thanks, but I'd better get back. I've left some notes at home that I need for the morning.'

'Ah well. At least let us see you into a cab,' Alex said.

'Always the gentleman,' said Sophie.

'OK, thanks,' Katie said, grudgingly accepting that maybe he wasn't all bad.

But when she got a text from Sophie twenty minutes later saying, 'As it's you, I checked. He is single, go for it,' her reply was prompt. 'Thanks sweetie but changed my mind. If he's scared by Decadence I'll terrify him. Shame – he's cute. Sure you can't overlook incest feeling? He's much more your type.'

She smiled at Sophie's response. 'Oh, Katie…' It was an in-joke between them – what Sophie always said to Katie when she overstepped the line. She texted back a quick 'Sorry babes – was just an idea. Big hugs and sweet dreams x' then started digging around in the bottom of her bag for change. She hadn't thought about the cab journey home when she'd insisted on settling the tab 'to celebrate your commission'.

'Still, Sophie's worth it,' she thought, breathing a sigh of relief as she found a ten pound note crumpled up in the bottom of her bag.

CHAPTER THREE

The Bet

Katie was finally enjoying a quiet night in, after spending a long Tuesday dealing with all the petty work problems that had arisen the day before. She'd turned up early to explain the various client 'issues' to her boss, Gemma, and had been surprised by how understanding she'd been. From then on the day had been easy, and she'd managed to leave work on time, cook herself seared honey and soy duck breast with potatoes dauphinoise, and have a long indulgent bath, all before 8pm. Now she was taking advantage of her rare night in to catch up on phone calls. Ved, of course, being the first person she called.

'So there I was, being all nice and inviting him along to Decadence and the arrogant wanker threw it back in my face.'

'Well, it's not for everyone, sweetie,' he said.

'If he'd just said that then I wouldn't mind so much,' said Katie, secretly thinking, 'Yeah, right. Anyone who isn't a prude would give it a go.' 'But he called us all perverts.'

'You say that like it's a bad thing,' Ved laughed. 'I'm a pervert and proud.'

'It was the *way* he said it though. Like he was judging me. Judging *us*. Doesn't that piss you off? What right has he got to do that?'

'Sounds like he got under your skin. Are you sure you don't want to fuck him?'

'God no. I mean, the packaging's nice but the sex would be so boring. If I wanted a once-a-week suck and fuck I'd have stayed with Stuart.'

'Just because he's not into fetish clubs, it doesn't mean that he's going to be dull in the sack. Maybe he just likes to keep his kinks to himself.'

'No, you don't get it. If you'd have seen how sneery he was you'd know he's never had proper sex in his life: probably not even had a finger up his arse.'

'Oh, darling, you really are missing a very important point here.'

'What's that?'

'Have you never converted a virgin?'

'God, who wants to go back to that: some bloke who comes in thirty seconds because he's so grateful to finally get laid. Anyway, he's 34. I'm sure he's not a virgin.'

'Not an *actual* virgin. A kink virgin. If you play them properly, they get *so* enthusiastic and you can get them to play exactly the way that you want them to in no time at all. I mean, look at what I turned you into…'

Katie felt her pussy muscles pulse as Ved lowered his voice into the 'dirty talk' tone that she knew and loved.

'Well, yes, but I was open-minded to start with.'

'Sweetness, you're not the first person I've helped "acclimatise". I do pull in the real world too. Trust me, a corrupted virgin makes for the dirtiest fuck around.' He paused, deliberately. 'Of course, you do have to have a certain amount of experience to turn them. Maybe I'm assuming too much of you. You are quite new to the scene, after all.'

Katie bristled at the implication. 'And have I ever backed down from anything you've suggested? I'm just as capable of corrupting someone as you are.'

'In that case, may I suggest a small wager?'

It was Katie's turn to pause. She'd been set 'wagers' by Ved before and they always pushed her limits – though she'd enjoyed every one. She was just constantly worrying about what he was going to suggest next when they played because she never knew quite what was going on in his kinky mind, and she was scared at the darkness he unleashed in her own.

'Go on…'

'Snare him. If you're so convinced that you can corrupt him, go for it. If you manage it, I'll be your slave for 12 hours. Anything you want me to do, I'll do it. But if you're not skilled enough to harness the kink within him, you have to be my slave for the night instead. Oh, and just to make it more interesting, let's go with no limits and no safe words, regardless of who wins.'

Katie pulled the receiver away from her mouth so that Ved wouldn't hear her nervous gulp. Despite her bravado, she knew that Ved was infinitely more hardcore than she was and would demand things of her body that he never had before. She had a vague idea of what that might be too, and the idea made her squirm – albeit as much in lust as in fear.

Then again, she had to admit that the prospect of having Ved at her beck and call was appealing. She'd often talked to him about dominating him and somehow he'd always managed to get out of it. She brought the phone back to her lips.

'OK. How long have I got?'

'Well, the longest it's ever taken me to convert a newbie has been a month. I wouldn't expect you to do better than me, so how does that work for you?'

A month was no time. Katie wasn't entirely sure that she had it in her to change a man's mind that quickly. Then again, it would give her something to focus on while Sophie was working on her painting. And she guessed that Sophie would be grateful to her for getting Alex out the house so that she could work. Although she was too polite to say it, Katie knew that Sophie always found it much harder to paint when there were other people around. Before she could convince herself to back down, the words were out of her mouth.

'Deal. I look forward to having you on your hands and knees in front of me, doing everything I tell you to.'

'Keep hold of that fantasy, babe. It's the only way you're going to get to see me like that. I look forward to seeing *you* in… well, in whatever situation I choose to put you in. I'm not going to warn you about what to expect. Much more fun to let that deviant little mind of yours conjure up all manner of horrors instead.'

With a wicked laugh, Ved hung up the phone.

Katie hated him for getting the last word, even if she was already beginning to feel horny at the meanderings of her mind. He certainly knew how to make her wet.

It was only when she was lying in bed, much later, that she realised she'd accepted a bet to seduce a man she'd been convinced she hated only a few hours before. 'Still, a bet is a bet,' she thought, as she tried to get to sleep, wondering exactly how she was going to win, but somehow finding her mind drifting to images of what would happen if she lost.

❧

The next morning, Katie's mind was made up. She was going to go for it – but not quite yet. Although she didn't *really* want Ved to win and get the upper hand, she knew that she had to take her time if she was to stand any chance of success. Vanilla or not, Alex was male and appearing over-keen wasn't going to do her any favours. She was tempted to pick Sophie's brain about exactly how she could pull him but, given how close she was to Alex, she couldn't guarantee that it wouldn't get back to him and turn him off. Instead, she avoided mentioning him to Sophie when they had their nightly phone-calls, and focussed on asking her about work. Unlike Katie, Sophie was a morning person so by the time Katie got home from work, she'd often already put in a 13-hour day.

'I don't know how you manage it,' Katie had said.

'And I don't know how you manage to party until 7am. I need to be tucked up in bed by midnight if I'm going to be good for anything the next day.'

Katie guessed it was just one of the differences between them.

It wasn't until Thursday that Katie dared to mention Alex's name to Sophie. She felt bad keeping her quest a secret but she knew that Sophie was too honest – and too close to Alex – to be able to keep a secret. Katie also suspected that she'd disapprove of the terms of the bet.

'So, I've been thinking…' she said.

'That sounds ominous.'

'Nothing bad. I just figure that I might have flown off the handle a bit with Alex when I met him. He's entitled to his opinion too. I mean, it's not like *you're* down at

Decadence with me every week and I love you to bits.'

'Don't worry about it. He certainly hasn't said anything bad about you.'

'Has he said anything about me? You didn't see the look he shot me when I snapped at him.'

'I knew it! You *are* interested in him. Well, I shouldn't really tell you this but he did describe you as my "gorgeous mad mate".'

'Mad?'

'He meant it in a nice way. Think you were just a bit full-on for him. The poor guy had only arrived from New York that morning. He was probably tired. I certainly didn't get the impression he thought badly of you. If he had, I'd have set him straight.'

'Oh God – sorry for being weird then. How about the pair of you come over to dinner on Saturday night so I can make it up to you? I promise I'll be nice. He'll get to see that I'm not just some dirty-sex obsessed bint.'

'I don't know about that,' Sophie laughed. 'But yeah, it'd be good to get out of the house. Every time I try to take a break here, I end up getting back to work within five minutes. I just feel so guilty about wasting time when I've got so little of it to get the job done.'

'Don't be daft, you need to take breaks or you'll burn out.'

'Says you, little miss workaholic. Then again, Alex is

like that. Actually, I think you two have got a fair bit in common. He's reminded me of you loads this week. He's certainly as into reading as you are – he was always a geeky kid but I thought he might have grown out of it. Think he's a bit frustrated by my book collection so maybe you can show him around your bookshelves.'

'Hell, whatever he wants to see, I'm happy to show him.'

'Oh, Katie…'

The pair laughed.

'OK, so shall we say seven – give us time to have a few drinks before dinner? And shall I invite someone else? Three is a bit of a weird number and I reckon you might get on with one of the guys I know from work.'

'God, I couldn't imagine anything worse – not that there's anything wrong with your job but come on, marketing men are all shiny suits and sales talk. And I haven't forgotten the last three guys you set me up with. Sometimes I wonder whether you know me at all.'

'I didn't realise Kev was into spanking when I set you up. And as to Dan, it's hardly my fault that you got so drunk together that he threw up on you – you could have paced things a bit. I still don't see what you thought the problem was with Leo.'

'He asked if he could borrow my underwear. To wear! You know the weirdest people.'

'Yeah, OK, but Jake isn't one of my clubbing mates. He's from work, the new guy, a 'creative'. He started in the design studio a couple of weeks back. Dark, stocky, Italian boy, late twenties…'

'And not a single brain cell.'

'Stop being so negative. He's not one of the "colourers in" if that's what you mean. He's seemed nice enough when we've been on fag breaks together. And I noticed him reading a book about Neville Brody in the pub at lunch the other day.'

Katie knew that a mention of Sophie's favourite graphic designer would do the trick.

'OK, you can bring him along if you insist, but please don't make it out to be some kind of a double-date thing. I don't want to get saddled with yet another one of your no-hopers. And I certainly don't want him to think that I'm desperate.'

'That'd mean I was desperate too, babe, and that's one thing I'm certainly not.'

'Whatever you say,' Sophie said, the humour obvious in her tone. 'OK, I'll trust you just this once, but you'd better not be bullshitting me. And if it just ends up being you, me and Alex that's no problem.'

'That's what you think,' thought Katie, as she hung up the phone. If things went to plan, she certainly didn't want Sophie in the way.

❧

Katie was in her own little world as she prepared the food for her 'seduction supper'. Her kitchen CD player was blaring out cheesy pop tunes as she chopped onions and celery finely, stirred the simmering stock and grated parmesan into a snowy tower. She'd decided to keep things simple: antipasta to start with, then artichoke heart risotto, and to finish a mango mousse with fresh raspberries. She opened the oven, standing back to let the heat dissipate before stirring the peppers, red onion, garlic bulbs and aubergine that were roasting in a balsamic and olive oil glaze. Everything was coming along perfectly. She opened the packets of parma ham, chorizo and mortadella, spreading them out on a big white plate, then drizzled them with white-truffle-infused olive oil.

Getting a wooden bowl from a cupboard, Katie ripped a French loaf into it in manageable portions – OK, ciabatta was more authentic but she found it a bit dry – and placed the bowl on the table, alongside extra virgin olive oil and aged balsamic for dipping. The fresh pink, orange and yellow gerberas she'd bought earlier lent a casual dash of colour to the table. Placing a bowl of rocket and parmesan salad next to them, and laying the table with funky pasta bowls, she was content with the way the table looked. Things were almost perfect but there was something missing. What was it? Ah, yes.

Katie lit a stick of her favourite Nag Champa incense, which mingled in a comfortable way with the tempting smells emanating from the cooker, and put on her favourite blues compilation. Pop was all very well for cooking but there was no way that she wanted to inflict it on the rest of the party: Sophie would be happy enough with it but she suspected the men would balk. As the instrumental intro came to an end and the seductive tones of Phoebe Snow lilted across the room, Katie smiled. 'At last, my true love has come along.' The words always got to her. But tonight wasn't about love. It was about getting what she wanted. And what she wanted, more than anything else, was to win her bet.

❧

Sophie and Alex arrived first, and were already most of the way down a bottle of cava by the time Jake turned up twenty minutes later.

'Jake, good to see you,' Katie said.

'Sorry I'm late – tube was a nightmare.'

'Thoughtless idiot,' Sophie thought. Politeness was important to her and despite her creativity, she was always punctual. Katie didn't seem to care though.

'Isn't it always? Drink? We've got some cava on the go,

or would you prefer a beer?'

'Cava's great, thanks. Chuck this in the fridge too.' Jake proffered a bottle of Jacob's Creek.

'A nice, safe choice,' thought Sophie. 'Still, at least he's polite enough to turn up with something, I guess.' Her mind flitted to her ex, Steve. He'd been the classic lad, more brawn than brain, with manners to match. Just taking a few cans of beer to a party was a push for him. He walked around expecting everyone to get out of his way, and always sat spread-legged, even scratching his balls in public on occasion. In the end the embarrassment had got too much for Sophie and she'd parted ways with him, albeit with a twinge of regret because, despite his bravado, he was a very sensitive lover. One thing that she did agree with Katie about was that size *does* matter, and he'd certainly got that box well and truly ticked. Since they'd split up a year ago, there hadn't been anyone else: she didn't see the point in casual sex just for the sake of it, and although Katie joked that she could spot Sophie's type a mile off, she hadn't met anyone who'd given her that 'flutter' for far too long, despite Katie's best efforts.

Now, watching Jake easily pop the cork on another bottle of cava that Katie had got from the kitchen, Sophie had to admit that he didn't seem as bad as the rejects Katie had set her up with before. In fact, if she was really honest, there was a distinct butterfly feeling in the pit of her stomach. He certainly looked right: as Katie had described, he was dark and swarthy with what looked like a six-pack underneath his T-shirt. His accent was somewhere between Leeds and Milan. The slight deadening of the Italian accent only added to his appeal: gave more humour to his voice. She always found pure Italian accents a bit too much of a cliché – like the owner was about to 'woo' her with 'cara mias' and 'bella bellas' that he'd used a million times before.

'This is my best mate Sophie, and her brother's mate, Alex,' Katie said, the introduction dragging Sophie out of her own thoughts.

'Pleased to meet you,' said Jake, shaking Alex's hand then turning his attention to Sophie. 'So Katie told me you're an artist. What do you work in?'

Sophie was impressed that he automatically focussed on her, rather than talking about himself as so many men are wont to do.

'Acrylics, mostly, although I've started experimenting with mixed media recently.'

'Really? That's what I went for for my degree show. I love the whole trial and error thing of seeing what works and what doesn't, mixing things up a bit instead of sticking to the same old same old.'

'Me too. In fact this painting I'm doing at the moment...'

As Sophie started to tell Jake about her latest commission – albeit skipping who it was for – Katie hid her smile. Her plan was coming together: she'd known Sophie for long enough to be able to spot if she was interested in someone, and there was definitely something going on. Sophie would never talk to a stranger that easily unless she was keen.

'Can you give me a hand dishing up?' she said to Alex, eager to leave Sophie and Jake together to enjoy their conversation.

'Sure thing,' he replied.

'I do hope so,' Katie thought, as she led him through to the kitchen.

ꙮ

Half an hour later, Katie was feeling content. Alex had proved himself to be a natural in the kitchen, helping her plate things up so that they looked their best and saying 'mind your back' when he walked behind her with the hot baking tray from the roast vegetables so that she didn't bump into him. Usually, she felt crowded when anyone else strayed into 'her territory,' as she saw the kitchen, but the proximity wasn't an issue with Alex. Perhaps it was just because of the bet spurring her on, but she definitely felt comfortable in his presence. Maybe getting what she wanted wouldn't be such a trial after all. 'Well, I did think he was cute before he opened his mouth,' she thought. 'And if he's this well trained in the kitchen, who knows how well trained I could make him in the bedroom.' Nonetheless, his earlier comments still rankled her and she had to bite her tongue when he commented negatively on the antique erotic prints on the wall: the Victorian etchings pictured sadistic men with handlebar moustaches whipping 'innocent' maidens, tall-booted Dommes towering over quivering gimps and, her favourite, a debauched orgy with alarming-looking phalluses entering holes of both men and women.

But instead of rising, she simply smiled and kept conversation deliberately light, talking about music, and asking him the best places to go in New York. In response, Alex was friendly, complimenting her on her taste in music, and making the right noises about the smell of the food. When they carried the starters through, Sophie and Jake were still immersed in conversation: it turned out that they'd shared a visiting tutor when they were studying, and they were busy reminiscing about his quirks.

'Remember the way he used to speak so slowly it was hell taking notes?' Jake said. 'In nineteen hundred...'

'...and forty...eight. God, yes. My pad was always littered with scribbled-out dates.'

Their insular conversation gave Katie the perfect

opportunity to get to know Alex a little better. Now they'd made small talk, it was time to kick-start her plan.

'By the way,' she said quietly when they sat down, 'I've been meaning to say, sorry if I was a bit full-on the other night. I'd had a hellish day at work so I wasn't in the best of moods.'

'Don't worry about it. I was probably a bit tetchy too. A seven-hour flight isn't the best preparation for a night out drinking. Shall we start again?'

'Cool. So tell me about you.'

It was always a killer question, Katie thought. Everyone loved talking about themselves. And as Alex started describing himself, she was more than happy to listen.

❧

The chink of cutlery on plates, as her guests tried to scoop the last vestiges of the mango mousse into their eager mouths, was music to Katie's ears.

'That was gorgeous, Katie. You're quite some chef,' said Alex.

Katie had to admit that his politeness *did* have a certain appeal.

'Thanks. I love cooking – I was thinking about going into catering if I didn't get the GCSEs I wanted, back in the day.'

'As if that was ever going to happen,' Sophie said. 'From everything you've told me, you were always going to go to university.'

'Well, yes,' Katie admitted. 'But back then I was so insecure I didn't take anything for granted. As it was I did some part-time jobs in restaurants when I was at uni instead, picked up a few tricks. It's all about buying the right ingredients really. Anyway, seconds for anyone or shall I clear up?'

She was met with polite murmurs of 'I'm stuffed' and 'I couldn't eat another thing'.

'Cool. Coffee then?'

'That'd be great,' said Jake.

'Mmm, yes,' said Sophie.

'I'll give you a hand if you want,' said Alex.

Normally Katie would have declined the offer – it was hardly a complicated task after all – but it gave her a chance to spend more time alone with Alex, and Jake and Sophie a chance to get closer. From the way that they were leaning towards each other, it was clear that the attraction was mutual.

'You two make yourselves comfortable on the sofa,' Katie said. 'Back in a min.'

And with that, she walked through to the kitchen, Alex following close behind.

'So, they seem to be getting on well,' Katie said once

they were out of earshot of the flirting pair.

'Yeah. He seems nice. And I'm pleased Sophie's got someone to talk to about art. I've felt guilty all week that I don't really know enough about it to talk to her properly. I mean, I'm happy to listen to her tell me about it but I can't really contribute to the conversation.'

'Sometimes listening is all a woman wants,' Katie said.

'You're just making me feel worse now. I've been talking about myself all evening to you.'

'You're interesting,' Katie said. 'I like hearing about you.' As she uttered the words, she was surprised to realise that she wasn't lying.

'Yes, but I haven't had a chance to find out anything more about you. Like, err, what's your favourite book?'

'Well, that depends,' Katie said. 'If it's one that I go back to time and time again, it's got to be *Hitchhiker's Guide to the Galaxy*.' She deliberately picked a book that she loved but knew scored highly with men too.

'That's one of my all-time favourite books,' Alex said.

'Bet you haven't read it as many times as me.'

'I dunno – it's got to be at least ten times by now.'

'Hmmm, OK, maybe you have then. I think I'm on about seven. Then again, you do have the benefit of nine years on me, old man.' Katie flicked a tea towel at him in jest.

'Cheeky cow. Anyway, it's not that much.' Alex picked

up a wet dishcloth and flicked Katie back, spattering her top with water. She noticed him glance at her breasts as she dabbed it ineffectually with her tea-towel. Progress!

'I'm 25, you're 34. You do the math,' she said, lapsing into a pastiche American accent.

'Actually, smart arse, I'm 33. Got put up a year at school for being bright. So nerr.' He stuck his tongue out at her.

'Oh, very mature. OK, eight years. What a difference. Gosh, you look so young and spritely compared to five minutes ago,' Katie said.

'You are *so* rude,' Alex said. 'Is this the way you always treat your guests?'

'Only the special ones. But if it's rude you want, I guess you might like one of my other favourite books.'

Katie was taking a chance by bringing sex into the equation but the physical flirtation – assuming he wasn't just treating her like a little sister? – made her prepared to take that risk. Alex raised one eyebrow.

'Oh yes?'

Relief flooded through Katie. OK, he *was* up for taking things up a gear. She had a chance of winning her bet.

'Yes.' Katie lowered her tone. 'If I want something to read in bed, it's got to be *Delta of Venus*.'

'I don't know that one.'

'It's by Anais Nin. I know you don't like sex but it's the most beautifully written erotica ever.'

'I never said I didn't like sex,' Alex said. 'It's just the pervy stuff that leaves me cold.'

'One man's meat…' Katie said, her gaze wandering down his body as she let her lips form the word 'meat', then glancing back up at him 'startled rabbit' style. 'I like to keep an open mind about these things. But I think you'd like Anais Nin. There aren't any gimp masks or handcuffs. It's just very evocative, words dripping from the page.'

'I do love good writing,' Alex said. 'OK, I'll give it a go. Just to prove I'm not as much of a prude as you think.'

'How about I read you one of my favourite bits later?' Katie said. 'I always think beautiful words sound so much better when they're read out loud.'

'I know what you mean. But it might be a bit much for a dinner party.'

'Well, if you want you are welcome to stay for a while. Sophie could probably do with some time alone with Jake. She's far too polite to say so but it might cramp her style if she takes him home and you're there.'

'You think they'll go back together tonight?'

As Sophie's laughter rang out from the next room, Katie leaned forward and whispered, 'I'd count on it.'

Sure enough, when Alex and Katie returned with coffee and Baileys, Sophie and Jake were snuggled up on the sofa rather more closely than was strictly necessary.

'Thanks, that's just what I need,' said Sophie. 'I'm beginning to get a bit sleepy.'

'I can see you home if you want,' Jake jumped in before Alex or Katie could speak.

'Well…' Sophie looked at Alex, as if for permission.

'Don't worry about me,' Alex said. 'There's still the washing-up to do and I promised Katie I'd help her out.'

'If you're tired, there's no need to stay just out of politeness,' Katie said. 'It is *me*.'

'And it gives me a chance to be on my own with Alex,' she tried to communicate to Sophie through a series of rapid eye movements. But Sophie was oblivious to all but her own desires, answering without even looking Katie properly in the eye.

'If you're sure, that'd be great. Thanks, Jake. I'll just finish my coffee and then we can go, if that's OK? I need my bed.'

As Sophie turned her gaze back to Jake, Katie suspected there wouldn't be a lot of sleeping going on that night.

❧

'Well, that went well,' said Alex, after Sophie and Jake had got into their cab.

'Yeah, I guess it did. Nice to see Sophie getting all sparkly over a bloke again.'

'Sparkly? You are a romantic deep down, aren't you?' said Alex.

'Never said I wasn't,' said Katie. 'On which note, you ready for this?'

She went to the bookshelf and pulled out her battered copy of *Delta of Venus*. She wanted to get in quick, in case Alex started to sober up and went off the idea.

'Why the hell not? Do you mind if I pour myself another Baileys?'

'Help yourself. Can you top mine up too?'

Katie flicked through the book as Alex sorted the drinks, eventually finding the bit she wanted: sensual without being graphic, she knew that the elegant prose would appeal to Alex.

'Shall we take a seat?' Katie gestured at the now-vacant sofa, and deliberately sat at a distance to Alex. She didn't want to make things too easy: he had to think that he'd seduced her, if she was to have her wicked way.

When she got to the end of the passage and looked up to see the shine in Alex's eyes – and his dilated pupils – she knew she had him hooked. He edged closer.

'Can you read me another bit? You've got a very sexy reading voice.'

Result! She turned to her favourite part of the book –

a much steamier extract. This time, Alex was silent when she reached the end. Then, 'Wow! That's incredible.'

And as Katie allowed her gaze to discreetly flicker over his body, she knew that it had had the desired effect.

'I know, it gets me every time. You can borrow it if you want.'

'Thanks. That'd be…great…I…' Alex looked into Katie's eyes, ignoring the proffered book.

'Lost for words? Who'd have thought it. Here you go.' Katie thrust the book at him.

Alex shook his head slightly, as if to clear out whatever thoughts were going through the mind, took the book and started leafing through it.

'Time for stage two,' Katie thought.

'Actually, I know this is really rubbish of me, but I've just come over really shattered. You know sometimes when it just hits you? Do you want to stay here tonight to give Sophie some time alone – they'll hardly have even got back yet.'

'I think I might do,' Alex said, the erotic words and alcohol combining to make him follow his base instincts. He leaned towards her and Katie knew that he was going for a kiss. She stood up.

'OK, well, the futon's a bit stiff. I'll give you a hand putting it up.' She stood up and gestured at the sofa he was sitting on.

'Err, OK,' said Alex, clearly confused.

'Bedding's in the basket in the corner. Help yourself to anything you want – there's orange juice in the fridge and Nurofen in the medicine cabinet if you start to feel hungover. See you in the morning.'

Katie gave Alex a hug, letting him briefly feel her body pressed against his, then headed for her bedroom.

'Always leave them wanting more,' she thought with glee, as she snuggled into bed, letting her hand wander down to finish the job that Anais Nin had started. She started imagining all the things she'd do to Ved when she won her bet but somehow, when she came, it was to the image of Alex's cock exploding in her mouth.

CHAPTER FOUR

Seduction

'Thanks so much for introducing me,' Sophie gushed. 'Jake's perfect.'

Katie sipped her latte, and tried to make sure that her grin wasn't too smug.

'So you had a fun night then?'

'Oh yes,' Sophie said. 'We talked for hours when we got back.'

'Talked?'

'Yes, talked,' Sophie said, with a mock-offended tone. She reddened slightly at Katie's 'yeah, right' gaze. 'OK, we did cuddle up a bit but that was it. And then he got a cab home like a gentleman.'

'Christ! I didn't realise men like that existed.'

'I know! Why do you think I was so insistent about meeting up? I need to pick your brains for tips. What's he like with women? How long's he been single for?'

'I thought you talked all night?'

'Yes, but I was hardly going to ask him stuff like that, was I? It makes me sound like a mad stalker.'

'Well, I don't know him that well but he certainly hasn't mentioned a girlfriend to me, or any ex, so I'm guessing he's fairly baggage free. Can't tell you much more than that, I'm afraid.'

'Lot of help you are. I guess I'll just have to find out for myself then. Christ, it's all so nerve-wracking, this relationship stuff. Feels like an age since I've felt like this.'

'Enjoy it. But actually, if you're after a confidence boost, I've got just the thing for you.'

'Oh yes?'

As Katie leaned closer to Sophie to share her idea, she knew she'd have to use every skill she'd learned in marketing to convince her – but that it was exactly the right thing to do.

❧

'I can't believe you talked me into this,' said Sophie, as they stood in the empty dance studio.

'Neither can I,' confessed Katie. 'But I promise you it's worth it. And see, I was right about the crowd, wasn't I?' She gestured at the other women in the room: a frumpy woman in her forties; a nervous-looking curvy 20-something; a couple of pairs of gossiping women who were clearly all mates; a raven-haired chubby goth; and a stunning, tall, 'perfect ten' woman of about 25, who was chatting away on her mobile phone.

'You mean it's not all perverts?'

'No – that you wouldn't feel out of place. You're at

least as sexy as all of them, and there's no way you can be as nervous as her.' Katie gestured at the curvy girl, who was chewing at the corner of her nail and shooting glances at the door. 'Come on, let's make her feel at home.'

She wandered over to the girl. 'Hi, I'm Katie. First time here?'

The girl nodded. 'I've just split up with my fiancé and I read an article saying that this would be a good way to boost my self-esteem, but now I'm not so sure.'

'Honestly, it's worth sticking out. I did the one-day course and it changed my life. It's Sophie's first time too so you're not the only one,' Katie said, bringing her friend into the conversation.

Sophie smiled at the nervous woman. 'I'm petrified as well. The things this one drags me into.' She waved a disparaging hand in Katie's direction.

'I'm glad I'm not the only one – we can stick together if it gets too scary, if that's OK with you?' The girl looked at Katie as if for permission.

'Sure,' Katie said. 'I don't need any hand holding.'

'I certainly do!' the girl said. 'I'm Lucy by the way.'

But before Sophie could answer, there was a tap, tap, tap of heels across the floor and a confident joyful voice ringing out.

'OK, girls, get into a nice line for me. I'm Lizzy Luscious.'

The group were immediately silenced by her friendly but authoritative tone.

As Katie looked at the relief on Sophie's face at seeing the tutor, she was glad she'd brought her along. She'd felt sure that seeing Lizzy – a woman in her forties with a rounded figure who was nonetheless one of the sexiest women she'd ever met – would be good for Sophie's confidence. Never the most body-confident person, Sophie tended towards paranoia when she started seeing a new man, and Katie had figured that a few sessions with Lizzy would soon sort that out.

'Today, I'm going to teach you the art of striptease,' Lizzy continued. 'Don't panic, you won't be getting naked quite yet. The *tease* is as important, if not more so, as the strip. So first of all, I'd like you to get into pairs.'

Seeing the look of fear in Lucy's eyes, Katie knew what she had to do.

'Why don't you two go together,' she whispered to Sophie. 'I can find someone else.'

'I'd rather go with you,' Sophie said. But when she saw how terrified Lucy looked at the idea of pairing with a total stranger, it was enough to change her mind. 'Oh, OK. See you later.'

Katie headed for the stunning tall woman, who despite her apparent confidence was standing on her own.

'Mind if I pair with you?'

'Sure.' The girl smiled. 'I'm Amber.'

'Nice to meet you. Katie.'

They shook hands, smirking at the formal gesture in such a surreal situation.

Half an hour later, the group had learned how to lick their lips sexily, look into someone's eyes while projecting sexy thoughts and walk slinkily. Katie was finding it relatively easy, courtesy of the day's training she'd done before, but was blown away by how well Amber was taking to it.

'This can't be your first time,' she whispered to her in between Lizzy's instructions.

'I'm actually a stripper,' Amber said. 'But I want to go off to the States and I've heard it's harder over there so I thought I'd get some practice in first. Up 'til now I've been self-taught.'

'You're clearly a very good teacher then,' Katie said. 'When you looked into my eyes I could have sworn you wanted me for real.'

'Maybe I did,' the girl teased.

'Maybe,' thought Katie. But she was pretty sure it was just flirting. Still, Amber was terribly attractive.

'Or perhaps I was just projecting,' Katie said, to let Amber know she'd be game if the offer was for real.

Sophie, meanwhile, was giggling with Lucy.

'I'm rubbish,' she said.

'Not as rubbish as I am. How do you do that turn

thing? You got it on first go. I thought I was going to fall over.'

'You just cross one foot in front of the other, then shift your weight onto the front foot and use that to twizzle around.' Sophie demonstrated the move. Lucy copied her, but had to take an extra step to complete the turn.

'No, like this.' Sophie repeated the move, just as Lizzy walked past to check on the girl's progress.

'Very good. You're a natural,' she said, smiling broadly at Sophie.

Lucy copied Sophie and this time got it right.

'Perfect,' Lizzy said. 'Practice the rest of the moves you've learned today for ten more minutes and then, if anyone wants to join me, I'm going to the pub. I always like to take my classes out after the session – gives you a chance to get to know each other.'

'Fancy it?' Sophie asked.

'That'd be great, thanks,' said Lucy.

By the end of the class, everyone was laughing together, watching themselves in the mirror as they walked, shimmied and gazed at their own reflections as if they were more of a sex goddess than Aphrodite herself.

'Fabulous, girls. You're doing brilliantly. So...' Lizzy turned off the CD player which had been blaring out sexy music. 'Pub time. But before we go, one last thing. Whip those T-shirts off.'

There was a brief pause in the laughter, then Lizzy whipped her own top off to reveal her own breasts, and show that she meant it. Amber followed suit, closely followed by Katie, Sophie, Lucy and the rest of the girls.

'Now shake 'em.'

And as Lizzy shimmied to make the tassels on her nipples twirl, her enthusiasm was infectious and everyone else copied her, albeit without tassels.

'See, there's nothing to it. Next week, I'll teach you how to remove your bras properly, so make sure that you wear one.'

Giggling filled the air once more, and when Lizzy put her top back on and told everyone to get changed, then follow her to the pub, there wasn't a single face without a broad smile on it. It was only as she left that Katie realised she hadn't even glanced at another woman's body: she'd been too busy watching herself in the full-length mirror to check that she was bouncing in the right way. 'Damn,' she thought, wondering what Amber looked like in the flesh. 'Ah well. Guess I'll get a chance to find out next week.' She hurried her pace to catch up with Sophie and Lucy who were nattering away, beckoning Amber, who was once more on her mobile phone, to follow.

❧

The girls were crowded round a table in a busy central London pub: Lucy and Sophie on one side, Katie and Amber on the other. The rest of the class were hanging on Lizzy's every word on the next table.

'That was amazing,' said Sophie, as she poured a glass of wine for Katie. 'Thanks so much for inviting me. I thought I'd hate it but it was really easy. Although I can't believe I got my boobs out. But I felt so comfortable that it seemed natural.'

'I know what you mean,' said Lucy. 'My fiancé would have laughed in my face if I told him I was doing something like this. I didn't even like having sex with the lights on – not that he ever complained. As long as he got to come he was happy. But that was kind of what made me do it. Doing something that I knew he wouldn't approve of, and certainly wouldn't think I was capable of.'

'So are you coming back next week to really rub his nose in it?' asked Katie.

'No,' said Lucy. As the girls looked surprised she laughed. 'I'm coming back next week because it was brilliant fun. How about you?'

'Oh yes,' said Katie.

'Me too,' said Sophie.

'And me, as long as it doesn't clash with one of my shifts,' said Amber.

'What do you do?' asked Lucy.

Katie enjoyed watching Lucy's eyes widen as Amber began to tell her about her job.

'I'm guessing that you're not exactly new to the strip scene then?' said Amber when Sophie and Lucy went to the toilets together later.

'I've been to a fair few events, yes. Though most of the striptease acts I know are through friends: met them at Decadence generally. Or through Ved Bergen – do you know him?'

'Know of him. He's got quite a reputation.'

'All justified,' said Katie. 'But he's adorable. One of my best friends.'

'Really?' Amber said, putting her hand on the back of Katie's. 'Tell me more…'

'Well, there was this time when he took me out on the pull with him. He decided that he wanted to have a reverse gang bang so I helped him pick up the women.'

Katie had been growing more enamoured with Amber as the evening had progressed and wanted to make it clear that she was up for playing not just flirting.

'Sounds like you're a talented woman,' Amber said. But as Sophie and Lucy returned to the table, she moved her hand away.

'So have you heard about Zena? They do the *most* amazing strip outfits there,' she said, taking conversation onto the safer ground of shopping, and leaving Katie with a definite feeling of unfinished business.

It felt like they'd been in the pub for mere minutes when the bell rang for last orders.

'Damn,' said Katie. 'Can't believe how fast the time's gone.'

'Me either,' said Amber. 'Shit! I'm going to have to shoot now to get the train back. But look, if you want, I'm playing at a club on Friday night. Why don't you come?' She pressed some fliers into Katie's hand and kissed her on the cheek, leaving a red lipstick print for all to see, then ran out the door, trailing her fake leopard-skin coat behind her.

'What do you reckon?' Katie handed a flier each to Sophie and Lucy, then started reading it to herself.

'Mistress Sinn's "Anything Goes" Spectacular: the ultimate in pole-dancing, striptease and grotesque burlesque, featuring Tawny Twilight, Poppa Cherry, Sunset Dream and Hidden Amber. All new Den of Delights.'

'Not my sort of thing,' said Sophie.

'You said that about this class,' Katie said.

'Yes, but this looks like Decadence and I was bored out of my mind there. No disrespect.'

'I'm not sure I'm quite ready for something like this yet,' said Lucy. 'But how about we go to dinner after next week's class, all four of us, if Amber is free? I lost contact with lots of my mates when I split up with Craig and tonight's been so much fun.'

'Definitely,' Sophie said, and they swapped numbers before heading off into the night to go home.

৵

The striptease class had been a welcome distraction for Katie, who was deliberately playing the slow game with Alex, waiting for him to call her. If she was going to bring him round to her way of thinking, he had to think that the seduction was his idea. Nonetheless, she was getting nervous when Wednesday rolled around and he still hadn't called. She'd felt convinced that he'd be on the phone by Monday night at the latest after her teasing behaviour on Saturday night. Didn't he realise that she was working to a deadline? 'Well, OK, I guess not,' she thought. 'But still, he *could* have called by now.' So it was with some relief that she picked up the phone on Wednesday night to hear his voice at the other end.

'Hi, it's Alex. Is that Katie?'

'Sure is.'

'Sorry I haven't called before now – been madly trying to get my life sorted over here and I kept losing track of the time and realising I hadn't called you when it was too late. I wanted to thank you for Saturday night. It was great. And…' Alex paused, clearly shy.

'Yes…'

'I was wondering if you fancied going out some time? I've nearly finished the book you lent me. And I'd be up for any other recommendations. You were right, it's beautifully written.'

'Sure. When you thinking?'

'How about tomorrow?'

'No can do, I'm afraid.' Katie had nothing more intensive planned than painting her nails but she didn't want to make things too easy for him.

'Friday?'

'Going out clubbing with mates and think it's going to be a big night so I don't think I'll be up for anything on Saturday. How about Sunday?'

'OK. Eight?'

'Perfect.'

'Is there any particular type of food you like?'

'Anything except Thai or curry,' Katie said. Actually, she was unfussy, but she didn't want spicy food to spoil the mood.

'French?'

'I adore French.'

'OK, how about I book somewhere and then drop you a text with the details once it's confirmed?'

'Great. Looking forward to it,' Katie said.

She hung up the phone, making a mental note to

ensure that any fun she had on Friday night was away from home. She didn't want to have to clear up after a heavy session on Saturday, and if Alex saw some of her favourite props lying around the place, he'd be scared off before things had even begun. Although… She logged on to her favourite beauty salon's website and fired off an email to book a bikini wax for Friday lunchtime. Some things worked just as well whether you were at a fetish night or with a perfectly vanilla guy.

❧

Lying back as the beauty therapist ripped the hairs from her most intimate parts, Katie tried not to cry. It was odd, she thought, how she could take a full-on thrashing while tied to the St Andrew's Cross but a bikini wax hurt so much more. She had to take a couple of aspirin before she went in just to be able to cope with it. Looking down at the end result, it was worth it though. She'd opted for having everything off, to give easy access. The first time she'd gone totally bare she thought it looked weird and was worried about it being overly child-like, but when she'd felt the difference it made to oral sex, she was convinced – at least enough to do it for special occasions. Some of her fetish friends had gone the whole hog and had their hair lasered off but she liked having the option to go for full muff, trimmed or nothing at all, not least because different men liked different things and she didn't want to limit her options.

Katie could hardly focus on work that afternoon, her mind alternating between thoughts of seeing Amber perform later that evening, and her date with Alex on Sunday. Eventually, she'd realised that there was only one way she was going to get any work done. She went to the loo and locked herself in a cubicle. Slipping her knickers off and putting them on the cistern so no one would see them and get suspicious, she ran her hand over the smooth skin, savouring the mild sting and heightened sensitivity from the waxing. Bringing her finger to her mouth, she licked it, then slid it down to rest on her clit, the wet pad of her finger rubbing against her hardening nub. As she rocked against her hand, she knew she was getting wetter and slid her finger further down to push just inside her entrance, closing her eyes and imagining that it was Alex's finger inside her instead. She pictured him kissing her hard, one hand around the small of her back and the other pushed into her knickers. It was working but something about it wasn't convincing: somehow she found her mind drifting to Amber instead.

Now *that* was easy to picture – Amber kneeling between her thighs in the toilets at the club she was going to later. Katie's movements got more vigorous as she imagined Amber gently parting her folds and holding her open so that she could lap at her clit and tongue-fuck her hole. She squeezed her own nipples hard, imagining that it was Amber reaching up to caress her instead. She knew she'd be enthusiastic, urging Katie on with demands to 'come on my tongue' and 'squirt over my fingers'. In just a couple of minutes of crude internal dialogue, Katie was coming around her fingers, biting her lip to stifle any moans that would give her away. After licking her finger clean, she pulled her knickers back up and went to check her reflection in the mirror. Other than a mild flush, there was nothing to give her away. She washed her hands to get rid of the smell of sex, and splashed water on her face. 'Nothing like an afternoon pick-me-up to restore focus,' she thought, as she walked nonchalantly back into the office, mind already buzzing with ideas for the project she was working on. In no time at all, her working day was over and she was ready to go home.

❦

Katie knew she'd picked the right outfit as soon as she walked into the club. Rather than going for fetish wear, she'd decided burlesque was a more appropriate look. Apart from anything else, it always drew more compliments from women and after her afternoon ménage à moi, she was in a Sapphic mood. Her tight lace corset was made from deep red silk, overlaid with vintage black lace. Her short bustled skirt flared out to show off her long legs, emphasised with seamed stockings. The outfit was finished off with Louis-heeled red satin shoes. She blinked, adjusting to wearing the false eyelashes – they always took her a while to get used to – and checked her red lipstick in her vintage compact. Perfect: classy slut – exactly the look she was after.

Looking around, she couldn't really see why the club was called 'Anything Goes'. Most of the women were dressed the same way as she was, and the men were suited, with barely a chin between them.

'Oh, Christ, fetish wannabes,' she thought, glad she hadn't brought Ved along as she'd considered. 'Just because they sometimes wank about threesomes and don't mind flashing a bit of flesh – no nips or bits though – they think they're so fucking cool.' She pondered that maybe that was the kind of club Alex had been referring to when he ranted about the fetish scene. From what she'd heard, New York had more pretenders than London.

'Still, at least I get to see Amber,' she thought, wandering up the stairs to find the stage.

The mood was quite different when she walked through the velvet curtains into the large upstairs room, with arches separating the various areas. The atmosphere was more charged, with women gyrating on three separate stages, one of which had a pole that Katie thought must be at least 30 feet high. On the first stage, a woman was clearly coming to the end of her act, bouncing up and down wearing nothing but a deep purple sequinned G-string and matching tassels, twirling them first one way, then the other, then in opposite directions at the same time.

The second, with the pole, seemed to be empty but as Katie passed through the first arch and drew nearer to it, she realised a woman was sliding down the pole at a pace, landing in perfect vertical splits to rapturous applause. Katie joined in, whooping, and triggering more whoops from the rest of the observers. That was quite some trick!

The third stage was at the back of the room, and Katie had to squeeze through the glittering crowd to see it, past women wearing lace and satin, sequins and pencil skirt suits; men in mod suits, smoking jackets and officer uniforms. The music changed as she moved through the room: from forties jazz in the burlesque area to dance music in the pole-dancing zone. And now, as she got through to the final stage, sleazy Nick Cave-esque sounds were projected, adding a dark edge that was only enhanced by the smell of heady incense and the fresh sweat of an aroused room of people.

Looking up at the stage, Katie could see why. Lights

were twinkling on a woman who was on all fours, stark naked, another woman between her legs licking her voraciously. Then she gripped the arse of the woman above her and pushed her face hard into her pussy, pulling back to reveal a string of beads between her teeth, which she was pulling out of the woman's hole. Wetness glistened on the large beads, and the woman on top was trembling in obvious arousal at the move.

After retrieving at least 12 inches of necklace, the woman clipped it around her neck, then returned to bury her face once more, this time in the trembling woman's arse. When she started to pull another necklace out, the crowd went wild. She took it slower this time, each bead taking what seemed like a minute to come out. By now the woman on top had moved her hand between her lips and was openly masturbating. Katie was impressed: this hadn't been what she'd been expecting when she saw the crowd downstairs. As the necklace came all the way out and the woman retrieving it stood up and clipped it around herself, the second woman emitted a scream of lust and fell forwards in what was obviously a genuine orgasm. It was only when she too stood up to take a bow that Katie recognised her as being Amber. 'The more I know about that girl, the more I like her,' she thought, walking towards the stage to catch Amber before she moved away.

'That was quite some act,' Katie said, when she finally

managed to work her way through Amber's admirers to the woman herself.

'Katie, babe. Good to see you. Glad you liked it. I'm on again in 40 minutes but do you fancy grabbing a drink backstage first? By the way, this is Nina.'

Katie recognised the woman who'd been pulling the – she now realised amber – beads from Amber's orifices. 'Hi,' she said. 'So how exactly do you land a job like that?'

'If you want it, I'm sure Amber will be happy to oblige,' Nina said, smiling at her but unable to mask the hint of bitterness in her voice.

Katie didn't quite know what to say, and was relieved when Nina stalked off muttering, 'I'm going to check downstairs and see if Lisa's turned up.'

'Is she OK?' she asked Amber.

'Oh, don't mind her. We're open. She's just pissed off because her new playmate's stood her up. Follow me.'

Katie did as she was told, enjoying the view of Amber's undulating arse under the silk robe that now clung to her slim frame.

Backstage wasn't quite what Katie had been expecting. There was a room just about big enough to hold a sofa and a table, one against each wall, a clothing rail balanced against the third wall and a long mirror running along the end. It was littered with underwear, open pots of glitter and bizarre props: a headless doll, some bloodied fake breasts and a stuffed parrot.

'Glamorous, eh?' Amber said. 'But at least it gives us somewhere to get away from everyone out there.'

As she spoke, a woman burst through the doors wearing nothing but a snake.

'Fuck, they're nightmares tonight. And Smoky shat all down my arm midway through my act.'

'Katie, meet Tawny Twilight – so called because she's a little bit dark. And Smoky – so named because when she first did her act with him, they nearly banned it,' Amber said.

'Hi. Err, sounds like you're having a rough night.'

'Ah, it's just one of the downsides of the job. I usually take baby wipes out with me but some fucker nicked them. Can I borrow one of yours?'

'Help yourself.' Amber waved her hand towards a leopard-print vanity case in the corner. 'Fancy some fizz?'

'I think I want to marry you,' Tawny said.

'Well, I'm already considering being otherwise engaged.' Amber winked at Katie. 'But if you're very good, maybe you can help us with our vows.' She popped the cork on the champagne and poured it into three plastic glasses.

'Sorry about the plastics.' She grimaced. 'Management bitch if we have real ones back here – worried about getting sued if one of us gets cut.' She handed Katie a glass then took a gulp from her own. 'Which is ridiculous really considering the act Tawny does later.' Katie watched as Tawny put Smoky back into his carrying case and reached into her bag to produce a string of razor blades. Her eyes widened.

'You don't…' She trailed off, unsure of how to phrase the question in case she was wrong.

'Shove them up my cunt. Yep. Wanna help? Amber has enough times before.'

Katie realised she was entering a whole new league and took a hefty swig of her champagne, relieved when Amber muttered, 'Don't scare the new blood' – then contradicted herself by asking Katie bluntly, 'So, do you prefer to fuck or be fucked?'

'Errr, fuck I guess.'

Katie felt embarrassed answering in front of Tawny but somehow she realised that she was being played, and Amber was dictating the rules of the game. Nonetheless, she'd had too many sub nights recently and was scared of exactly what Amber might expect of her if she let her take the lead.

Katie was glad that she picked the former option when she saw the size of the strap-on that Amber produced from her bag.

'Part of your act?' she asked.

'Oh no, strictly recreational. But there's so much

opportunity here that I always make sure I carry her.'

'Her?' Katie asked, wondering how a cock quite that big and thick could be feminine.

'Sure. She keeps going for as long as I want her to, and always makes me come. What man do you know like that?'

'Quite a few,' thought Katie, but she was pretty sure that Amber was militant sexuality-wise and didn't want to blow her chances, so instead she just laughed.

'Wanna try her?'

Although Katie had fucked a couple of men with a strap-on she'd never tried it with women, preferring to relish the chance to taste a woman's juices, and have a soft face buried in her own pussy. But hell, life was for living.

'Do you want me to?'

'I've been wanking about it ever since I saw you, sweet thing. Take off the skirt and underwear and step in.'

Amber held the harnesses in position for Katie to climb into. Katie did as she was asked, the heft of the toy giving her a strange feeling of power.

'OK, but if I'm going to fuck you then you're going to be fucked. We play my way from now on.' Katie looked at Amber for permission, despite her dominant words.

'Whatever you say, honey. Do with me what you will.'

Amber lay back languidly, looking at Katie through heavy-lidded eyes.

'In that case, spread your legs. Tawny, feel free to stay if you want.' Although Katie had felt uncomfortable at first, Amber's easy acceptance of her lent her confidence. 'And do feel welcome to join in.'

As she spoke, she hoped that the razor blades would stay well away from proceedings. Still, who knew, maybe it could be fun? Rather than let her mind wander through the various possibilities, she put herself to the task in hand.

'Open yourself up for me. I want to see your cunt.'

Amber moved her long fingers down to her pussy and parted the lips, pulling them wide to reveal a clit that was pierced with cute amber studs lining each side of her labia, and a final one on a ring through her clit hood. Katie refused to let herself show any surprise and instead, knelt to taste Amber's sopping pussy. Her tongue darted over the tip of her clit, pushing at the ring with her lips.

'Oh, honey,' Amber moaned, then settled back into contented moaning as Katie licked her fingers and pushed a finger each into Amber's pussy and arse, pistoning them back and forth as her tongue laved Amber's clit. She raised her head.

'You like that.'

'Honey, you have no idea… Please don't fucking stop.'

'I've got no intention of it.' She traced her tongue over each of Amber's piercings, then sucked lightly, worried to apply too much suction in case one of them came out.

'I can take more than that,' Amber whispered.

Katie moved up towards the ring once more and sucked it harder, extending Amber's clit out as her fingers continued to thrust in and out of her eager holes. She heard a moan from behind her and turned to see Tawny fingering herself.

'I've got two hands,' she said.

Tawny beamed at her and moved next to Amber on the sofa, spreading her legs to give Katie easy access to her pussy. Katie pulled her lips away from Amber for a moment, so that she could see well enough to easily slide two fingers of her left hand into Tawny's wetness without losing a single stroke of the fingers of her right hand in Amber's holes. She felt all powerful with a woman on each hand, both groaning at her ministrations.

Looking at the view in front of her – Amber lithe and tanned with brown-tipped small breasts and a shaved pussy, Tawny dark and pale with impressively red nipples topping full breasts, and a natural bush – she took a mental picture, knowing that she'd be reliving the moment again and again when she used her toy at home. She crooked the fingers of her left hand upwards to press against Tawny's G-spot, eliciting a squeal from the eager stripper.

'I should warn you, I'm a squirter,' Tawny said, which only made Katie redouble her efforts. She loved it when she made a woman ejaculate: there was something mystical about it compared to making a man come. She'd only managed to ejaculate herself a few times – always at Ved's expert hand – so was impressed by any woman who found it easy. She let her fingers rub up and down Tawny's sopping hole, feeling her G-spot swell with every thrust.

Meanwhile, Amber was begging for more. Katie slid another finger into her pussy but Amber moved her hand down to pull the fingers away, repositioning it at her arse. Katie immediately realised what she wanted, and slid it into her, in a swift move that she suspected would stretch Amber – but was pretty sure she'd like. She was beginning to suspect that Amber liked to play with pain and pleasure even more than she herself did. Sure enough, the move was rewarded by a breathy moan from Amber's lips and a flood of pussy juice over her fingers.

Tawny was beginning to gasp too, her breath coming in ever-faster, ever-deeper spurts. Katie could tell that she was drawing near, and pressed her two fingers firmly up directly into her, by now massively engorged, G-spot.

'Oh fuck,' Tawny moaned, tensing her thighs hard, and rewarded Katie with a clear spray of liquid squirting into her palm and up her arm. Katie kept her fingers in position until she was sure that Tawny had come as much as she could, then pulled them out of her and licked her palm.

'God, you're delicious,' she said, then, boldened by making Tawny ejaculate, added, 'and so am I. Want to find out?'

Tawny moved behind Katie, pulling the harness to one side to allow her access to her slit. She ran a lazy tongue up it, and Katie was shocked to realise that Tawny too was pierced. But how the hell was she doing *that*? She stopped, awed for a second, trying to figure out what was going on. Amber laughed.

'I think she's just noticed your split tongue, Tawny.'

As Tawny repeated the move, Katie realised what was going on. Tawny's tongue was split down the middle – each side pierced – and able to move independently from the other. The feeling was bizarre, having both sides of her clit licked at the same time but a different rhythm – like being licked by two women at once, but without the complicated positioning that was usually required. It was certainly a night for new experiences. She shifted focus back to Amber again, fingers thrusting and tongue matching pace with Tawny's flickering. But by now her tongue was getting tired – and she wanted to take things up a gear.

'Bend over the sofa. I want to fuck you while Tawny licks my cunt,' she ordered Amber, who all too willingly obliged. Katie positioned the head of the strap-on at Amber's cunt and, with one long, slow thrust, buried herself inside her, making Amber feel every one of the ten inches of the toy as it slid into her sopping depths.

'Ohhh, honey,' Amber moaned as she started to thrust back and forth. Tawny, meanwhile, had moved to lick Katie's arse, the two sides of her tongue flickering around the outside, giving Katie a whole new sensation to enjoy, that only got the more intense when Tawny slipped one side of her tongue into her arse while the other expertly rimmed her. Now it was Katie's turn to moan, then thrust harder into Amber, grabbing her hair and pulling it back hard as she fucked her.

'You going to come for me, bitch?' she snarled, amazed at the persona that was taking her over.

'Fuck my arse,' Amber said, 'and I will in seconds.'

Katie didn't think she'd be able to take the massive toy but guessed that Amber knew her own limits, so leaned forward to slick Amber's arse with saliva before pressing the toy against her willing hole. This time, she went even more slowly, determined not to hurt her new playmate, trying to block out the sensations coming from her own nether regions courtesy of Tawny's improbable tongue. But Amber clearly wanted it hard and fast, and pushed back against Katie, slamming onto the giant cock, fingers moving between her thighs as they had on stage. She was yelping by now, hips jolting back and forth against Katie's hips, banging into her so hard that Katie could feel her clit start to bruise. Then, with one almighty final thrust,

Amber screamed that all-too-familiar scream, before flopping forward onto the sofa, gasping heavily. Katie felt a massive rush of endorphins: she'd made this gorgeous woman come – with her cock.

She pulled it out, then moved away from Tawny so that she could remove the strap-on to give her full access to her pussy. She lay flat on her back, not caring about the lingerie that was scattered on the floor beneath her. She wanted to come – now. Tawny took the hint and pushed her face into Katie's pussy, sliding her fingers into her and letting that tongue roam over Katie's clit in a way she'd never felt before. She closed her eyes and replayed the moment that Amber had come in her head as she enjoyed Tawny's touch, triggering her own orgasm in a matter of minutes. As she shuddered into Tawny's face, Tawny echoed Katie's earlier move and pressed her fingers hard against her G-spot. Katie felt a massive release, and when she looked down at Tawny's face, she saw her smiling broadly, face dripping with ejaculate.

'I guess there's no need to ask what's been taking you three so long,' hissed Nina from the door. 'Amber, they've been calling for you for the last ten minutes. Gav says if you don't get out there right fucking now, you're fired.'

With an apologetic glance to Katie, Amber hurriedly pulled on a chainmail dress, and took a metal dildo with amber studs from her bag.

'See you on Monday,' she mouthed to Katie, as she followed Nina out of the dressing room.

'Don't mind Nina,' Tawny said once she was out of earshot. 'She's a fucking nightmare. I keep telling Amber to dump her but she never listens.'

Then she moved up Katie's body and gave her a long wet kiss, before saying, 'If you ask me, she'd do a lot better with you. Then again, I'd quite like to keep you for myself.'

Katie pulled Tawny into another kiss. She was still in awe at Tawny's tongue and wanted to experience it every way she could.

❧

The next morning, Katie was feeling less than on top form. She'd ended up partying with Tawny until dawn, only taking breaks to watch her perform her shocking set. True to her word, Tawny had pulled the string of razor blades from her pussy in front of an awed crowd. She'd also fired ping-pong balls over their heads and culminated by pouring a pint glass of what looked like blood into her pussy then squirting it out to soak the crowd. Even Katie had felt squeamish watching that particular move, but then again, she suspected that Tawny's limits went well beyond those of even her wildest fetish friends. She'd have to introduce her to Ved. It'd be interesting seeing which one of them balked first. In fact, she thought, it might be fun to take Tawny with her when she won her bet. Which she really had to start planning.

To start with, though, she was going to take a long salt bath. After the pounding her pussy had taken the night before, she needed to give it some TLC if it was going to be in any state to use on Alex. She took the phone into the bathroom with her. She was pretty sure that Ved would want to know every detail of her sordid soiree and wanted to tell him all about it before she forgot a single second of the night.

❧

Ved had been surprisingly quiet when she told him about her night with Amber and Tawny. Katie guessed that he was worried that she was catching him up. He did like to be the one who corrupted her. When she'd told him about Tawny's tongue, she'd heard something in his voice that she'd never encountered before: jealousy. Whether it was because she was having fun without him or that she'd experienced something that he hadn't, she wasn't sure – though she suspected that it was the latter, given that he usually demanded to know all about her 'extra-curricular' fun.

She smiled at the thought of him acquiescing to Tawny's touch: she'd mentioned the idea to her, though skipped the part about the bet, and Tawny had been keen to meet him. His infamy certainly made it easier for her to find willing playmates for them in the fetish scene, and because Tawny had confessed that she'd fuck blokes but never date one, Katie didn't feel jealous at the idea of sharing Ved with her. Maybe they'd lick his cock together, one on either side of him, but deny him orgasm, as he'd denied her on so many occasions: she knew that it would be damned near impossible for him to hold back when he saw – and felt – Tawny's tongue, which would only make it more fun. Hmmm. So many games to play. She turned over a few possibilities in her mind – collaring him, spanking him, maybe even dressing him up in her clothes to truly humiliate him – but then stopped herself. 'Don't count your chickens,' she rebuked herself. 'You've got to get Alex first.' She turned her attention to her wardrobe. So, what to wear for the big seduction? 'Simple and classy,' she thought. 'And easy to remove.'

The lilac silk dress clung flatteringly to Katie's figure as she walked down the street towards the restaurant. Alex had offered to pick her up but she'd declined, wanting to make an entrance instead. The bias cut of her dress meant that it swirled as she walked, giving her a girlish look that was tempered only by the strappy silver five-inch heels that made her legs look as if they went on for ever. It was a balmy evening so she'd skipped stockings, instead applying a light layer of fake tan to her skin. Her make-up was understated but she'd curled her hair so that it fell in loose ringlets around her face. The antique silver necklace with a fire opal pendant and matching dangling earrings offered the perfect elegant finishing touch.

As she walked into the restaurant, she knew that she'd dressed to perfection. Alex froze, clearly stunned. It took him a few moments to rearrange his features then, 'Wow! Katie, what can I say but…wow! You look absolutely incredible.'

'You look pretty good yourself,' she said, impressed at the sight of him in a slim-fitting dark suit, and dark green shirt.

'So, can I get you a drink?' he asked.

'That'd be lovely.'

Alex pulled out her chair for her, and Katie sat down, content that the evening had started exactly the way that she'd hoped. Despite her passion for being tied up and humiliated, there was something to be said for being treated as a lady. Perhaps winning her bet was going to be more fun that she'd first thought.

By the time their starters arrived – French onion soup for him, smoked duck breast salad for her – Katie and Alex had already established a lot of common ground. As well as a shared passion for books, their sense of humour was near-identical – dry and cynical with the occasional burst of childlike silliness – and they had similar tastes in music – no mean feat given that Katie loved an eclectic mix of indie, jazz, and soul, 'but not that modern shite that pretends to be soul and just bangs on about shagging "hos"– Aretha Franklin, Al Green, Jimmy Cliff – proper stuff.'

'I couldn't agree more,' Alex said. 'Though Etta James is my favourite.'

'I'm impressed,' Katie said.

'I thought it'd take a lot more than that to impress you,' Alex joked.

'I'm just an old-fashioned girl at heart,' Katie said. 'I mean, that music's got real romance to it, real heartbreak, real emotion.'

Although she'd planned on using the 'old-fashioned girl' line to seduce Alex – the virgin/whore complex was so common that she often played up to it – Katie realised that she wasn't lying to him. She *did* like the evocative lyrics, and when she'd first split with Stuart she'd sobbed herself to sleep listening to 'Tracks of My Tears' more times than she cared to remember.

'You're not the person I expected you to be when we first met,' Alex said. 'I thought you were some scary Domme type.'

'Not at all,' Katie said, but his words jolted her out of their easy banter. Instead, she found herself picturing Ved on his knees, licking her pussy while she trained a whip over his pert arse. She didn't want to get too into Alex, she reminded herself. This was about a bet and nothing more. 'Still,' she thought, as Alex deliberately placed his hand on top of hers on the table, 'at least it looks like I'm in with a good chance of winning.' She put down her fork so that she didn't need to move her hand from underneath Alex's, and topped his glass of wine up. She suspected it would 'provoke his desire'. She just hoped it wouldn't lessen his performance.

It didn't take long for Alex to drag Katie's attention away from Ved once more. He'd started talking about Eddie Izzard and soon they were swapping favourite lines, and laughing away. They hardly noticed the waiter take away their starters and replace them with the main courses.

'Try one of these,' Katie said, dragging a scallop through the exquisite pea sauce on her plate, and adding a crisp piece of bacon and chunk of black pudding. 'It's amazing.'

Alex obediently opened his mouth, eyes wide as he

savoured the tasty mouthful.

'That's fantastic. Try this.' He followed suit, slicing a piece of rare beef and adding a miniature chunk of horse-radish-crusted crisp potato.

'God, I don't know which is better,' Katie moaned.

'That's one of the things I love about being with a woman who enjoys her food – sharing it.'

'In that case,' Katie said, as she swept a scallop into her own mouth, 'how about we go for a sharing dessert plat-ter? It's incredible.'

'I'm not usually one for sweets,' Alex said. 'But who am I to deny you?'

There was a distinctly flirtatious tone in his voice, and Katie was pleased to note he squeezed her thigh under the table as he spoke. She thought she saw him catch his breath when he realised she was bare-legged so he was touching her soft skin.

'I'm sure you'll love it as much as I do,' she said, her tone similarly husky to his own.

Sure enough, when the platter had arrived packed with lavender-scented crème brulee, hot chocolate brownie with white chocolate ice-cream, fresh profiteroles stuffed with strawberries and cream instead of the usual crème patisserie and topped with a decadent chocolate sauce, and the most delicate crisp tarte tatin Katie had ever tasted, Alex had dived in. But once he'd loaded his fork with a chunk of brownie and generous spoonful of ice-cream, he'd proffered it towards Katie.

'Ladies first.'

She took the mouthful from his fork and moaned at the rich flavours.

'Better than sex,' she said.

'Really? In that case there's hope for me yet. I've never tasted a dessert that's better than sex.'

But as Katie returned the favour and filled Alex's mouth with the sensual dessert, he had to concede, 'OK, it *is* better than *bad* sex.'

They laughed, and continued to feed each other dessert, spoonful by spoonful. By the time the bill arrived – which Alex insisted on paying – neither of them was in any doubt that they'd be spending the night together.

❧

Back at Katie's flat, the tension was palpable. She'd set her iPod to randomly select tunes from her 'soul' folder, lit candles and made a cafetiere of coffee, which she'd carried through along with two shots of sambucca and a few coffee beans. Although she'd been tempted to just pounce on Alex, she wanted him to be the one to make the first move – but she had no problem with making the atmosphere as conducive as possible.

'Put one of these between your teeth, then down the sambucca,' she said, in answer to Alex's quizzical look at the coffee beans.

'Are you trying to get me drunk and take advantage?'

'Would I do a thing like that?' Katie said, as she took a coffee bean between her teeth and knocked her sambucca back.

'I think you might,' Alex said. 'And I don't think you'll get any objections from me.'

He downed his own drink, then removed the coffee bean from between his lips.

'You're supposed to crunch it,' Katie said, though her own one was still intact.

'Yes, but then...' Alex said, slipping his fingers into her mouth to retrieve her bean, '...I'd have a mouthful of grit when I did this.'

He pulled her to him and pressed his warm alcohol-tinged lips to hers. Katie was shocked at the instant chemistry, but let Alex set the pace, his lips first soft against hers, then firmer as he snaked his tongue between her lips. She focussed on enjoying the sensation rather than kissing him back, not moving her tongue into his mouth until her body refused to let her hold back any more. When her tongue finally touched his, Alex moaned, first pressing his body against hers as she deepened the kiss, then pulling away.

'That's lovely,' he muttered, lips mere millimetres away from hers, before tangling his hands in her hair to pull her back towards him once more.

This time the kiss was more intense, tongues fiercely lashing each other. Lost in the moment, Katie felt her head start to swim with sensation. Her hands gripped Alex's back, nails digging into his shoulder-blades as he alternated hard and soft pressure, teasing pecks with cunt-melting passionate kisses. Breathy moans filled the air – whether hers or Alex's Katie couldn't quite tell – and their bodies pressed ever-closer. By now, Alex was running his hands over her body, from the swell of her breast to the sensitive curve of her lower back. When he took her hand and placed it on his jeans, saying 'see how much you turn me on?' Katie felt an impressive and extremely hard bulge. The audacity of the move from someone so unexpected gave her a surprising blast of lust. She stumbled to her feet and grabbed Alex's hand.

'Come to bed.'

Even though she'd been determined not to initiate any contact, Katie wanted Alex too much to care. Her skin was tingling so much that she was trembling with every touch of his fingers, and she knew if she didn't stand up soon, she wouldn't be able to because her legs were starting to shake.

Alex answered by standing and giving her a kiss that Katie was sure she'd remember for ever: his arm hooked around her waist and she could feel herself being pushed backwards Scarlett O'Hara-style as his pelvis pressed to hers, stamping his arousal against her flesh. His tongue flickered this way and that, hands now pulling her hair with more force, tilting her head back and making Katie whimper with pleasure. 'It was all an act,' she thought, as he ground his hard cock against her 'He *is* into kinky sex. I've won.' But all thoughts of the bet were dashed from her mind as they stumbled, lips still touching, into the bedroom, and she thought she felt his hand slap her smartly across the face mid-kiss. It was so shocking, so intimate, something she'd only let Ved do once so taboo was the act. Maybe it was her imagination? As Alex pulled her dress over her head to reveal her naked but for heels and necklace, and buried his face in her neck, kissing her so languorously that she thought she was dreaming, she was sure that it must have been. Someone so tender could never be so base. She surrendered herself to the delicate sensation of his lips running up and down the soft skin of her neck. Only when Katie was begging him to touch her more intimately did Alex finally move from trailing his tongue lingeringly over her neck, gently nibbling her and letting his lips play over the sensitive spot where neck meets shoulder. She'd thought she was going to come from that alone, but when he moved to suck one nipple lightly into his mouth, toying with the other one between finger and thumb, she was glad she hadn't. She sank down onto the bed, pulling him with her, and couldn't help from mewling his name as his lips explored every last inch of her skin. When he finally reached her dripping core, she almost came at first touch, but he pulled away.

'I want you to wait to come until I'm inside you. I want to feel you coming around me. Is that OK?'

Although it was a request rather than an order, it was even harder for Katie to hold back her climax than it had been in the fetish club mere weeks before. But Alex was making her feel so good that she didn't want him to stop, wanted to make the feelings last for ever. She nodded her acquiescence and relaxed her muscles in the hope of containing herself.

Alex's tongue languidly circled Katie's clit, teasing it to a stiff bud, then retreating to focus his attentions lower down. He darted it in and out of her wetness, pausing only to tell her how incredible she tasted, then returned to her clit and started lapping it in a slow and steady pace. Katie knew that she was going to explode if he didn't stop soon, and reached down to pull him away from her. He resisted for a second, giving her a few last rapid licks, then let himself be pulled upwards.

Pushing Alex onto his back, Katie kissed him lingeringly as she undressed him, enjoying the taste of her own juices in his mouth. Now it was her turn to pleasure him.

She worked her lips down his body, sucking his beautifully shaped cock into her mouth. It was large, rock hard, and the well-defined head on top of the thick shaft was a joy to behold. She could feel herself getting wetter just by looking at it, and when she tasted the clean salt-sweet skin, and felt it harden ever-more in response, she moaned in pleasure. Her tongue laved softly over the sensitive tip, then she sucked him right down to the back of her throat before softening the suction and lapping her way back up to the tip.

Katie cupped Alex's balls in her hand, teasing them like Chinese stress balls, tugging them lightly as she felt them tighten. Her saliva coated his cock, making it easy for her to move her hand up and down his shaft, wanking him into her mouth. His pre-cum was sweet, making her crave the taste of his cum, but her pussy was pulsing, desperate to be fucked: she knew she had to have him inside her soon. Alex clearly felt the same way, and she heard the rip of a condom packet just as she felt his cockhead begin to pulse in the back of her throat. She pulled away: there was no way she wanted to waste his orgasm down her throat, no matter how much she wanted his cum. She needed to feel his cock in her right now.

Alex slipped the condom on with ease and in one swift move, flipped Katie onto her back and slid his cock right up to the hilt, making her squeal half in pleasure, half in pain. She raised her legs up onto his shoulders, wanting to feel him even deeper inside her, to take her, to own her. She wasn't sure if she was just thinking it or actually saying the words out loud but either way, he seemed to know what she wanted, and pounded into her, gathering her hands up to pin them over her head as he rode her hard and deep.

Katie could feel herself getting wetter with every thrust, and clenched her muscles around him, eager to feel him coming inside her, knowing it would trigger her own orgasm if he did. Alex leaned forwards and kissed her roughly, lips pressed hard to hers, teeth biting into the tender skin of her lower lip. She bit back and was rewarded with him pushing even deeper inside her and, she was sure, mutter 'filthy bitch'. Katie arched her back, trying to open herself up to Alex, to take him further inside her than any man had ever gone before. She heard him gasp as she moved her hips back and forth, matching his every thrust.

Before long, she felt the pressure start to build up in her pelvis: a warmth spreading through her most intimate parts, a steady heartbeat start to go in her clit. She knew she was going to come any second now and tried to cling on but it was no good. As Alex thrust inside her once more, she felt him pressing hard against her clit and started convulsing around him. The muscular contractions around his cock sent Alex over the edge and, face twisting into a silent scream, he came inside her, the rhythmic pulses extending Katie's own orgasm until she was lost in a world where all that existed was pleasure, all that mattered was sensation, all that she was was orgasm. Her eyes were tightly closed, as if trying to keep the outside world from intruding on her pleasure, trying to make the feeling last for ever. She suspected from his heavy breathing that the feeling had been just as intense for Alex.

As the pair floated back down to earth, Alex leaned forward to peck Katie tenderly on the forehead.

'I know I said it earlier but, wow! Just…wow! You're incredible, Katie. Just let me get rid of this…' He gestured at the condom and stood to go to the bathroom. '…and I'll be back to give you the hug you deserve. Do you want any water or anything?'

'That'd be great, thanks. Glasses are…'

'…in the cupboard to the right of the sink. I remember from the dinner party. Back in a sec.'

He walked out of the room, clearly comfortable with his nakedness.

Katie lay back in contented bliss.

'Well, that was a pleasant surprise,' she thought. 'So much for vanilla. Hair-pulling, face-slapping, pinning me down, dirty talk… I think I have a Dom on my hands.' The thought made her smile. OK, so maybe he wasn't quite ready for public performances yet, but she was sure that he'd be happy to indulge her at Decadence in front of Ved, once she'd shown him quite how good a slave she could be.

But as Alex came back into her room, and put his arm around her, all thoughts of Ved vanished. Nestled on his chest, Katie breathed in his scent: fresh sweat mixed with Chanel Pour Monsieur – she'd had to ask what made him smell so good earlier in the evening. Relaxation flooded through her, and she felt content and sated. Or *almost* sated, she thought, as she turned her back on Alex and he moved to spoon her, his cock stiffening as it nestled between her buttocks. Katie wriggled against him, enjoying feeling him rise against her skin, and as Alex dropped his lips to her neck once more, and started kissing her and whispering lascivious 'nothings' in her ear, she decided she was more than happy to go for round two...

CHAPTER FIVE

Submission

Walking home the next morning, Alex was so happy that he was scared he might start whistling. It had been quite some night. He'd been dubious about Katie at first, with her talk of pervy clubs, but Sophie had sworn that she was a lovely person once you got to know her. He was glad he'd given her the benefit of the doubt. She might talk the talk but once he'd been back at her place there wasn't a pair of handcuffs or spanking paddle in sight. She just liked a good old-fashioned fucking – and he'd been more than happy to oblige. His mind drifted to his morning wake-up call of her lips around his cock, but he had to shake his head to clear the image: he could feel himself stiffening at the memory and he had a long walk home.

Alex had considered getting the tube but it was a gloriously sunny day and he was feeling so positive about life that he'd decided the walk would be good for him. He could probably do with the exercise too, if he was going to be able to deal with young Katie's demands. Although he was by no means unfit, his muscles were aching after a thoroughly demanding night. Every time he and Katie had tried to drift to sleep, one or the other of them had got aroused again and, in turn, given the other one the horn.

In the end, it was only because they'd run out of condoms that they'd finally gone to sleep.

He wondered if it was too soon to text Katie. OK, so she'd been the one who'd led him to bed but Sophie had warned him that she was a heartbreaker. He hadn't been expecting anything more than a bit of fun, to be honest – after his break-up with Angela, a relationship was the last thing on his mind. But he'd been surprised by how well the pair of them had clicked. Katie had a wicked sense of humour, and he suspected she wasn't as tough as she made herself out to be. More to the point, she sucked cock like a dream. A very, very wet dream. He decided to wait until the end of the day. He didn't want to scare her off, but he didn't want her to think he'd lost interest now they'd had sex either.

❧

When Katie got Alex's text, she breathed a sigh of relief. She'd been worried that he wasn't going to call – you could never tell, no matter how keen someone seemed at the time – but the message was suitably reassuring.

'Thanks for a great night. Can't believe how sore I am though. Few sessions at the gym before next time, I reckon. How's Wednesday?'

She waited for an hour before replying – not wanting

him to think her too desperate – with a simple message.

'For gym or for another workout? Either way, be good to see you hot and sweaty. Weds good for me.'

Minutes later, Katie's phone rang. 'Alex', read the screen. She toyed with letting it go through to voicemail but her desire to talk to him got the better of her.

'Hi gorgeous,' she said, and a few minutes later, they'd arranged their next date.

The second date was even better than the first one: a trip to the cinema followed by a night at his place. Sophie had gone away for the evening, although she hadn't said where. Katie suspected that Jake was involved, though she'd avoided asking him about Sophie when she was at work, for fear of getting stuck in the middle if things went wrong. Once back at the house, it had taken mere seconds before Alex had bent her over the sofa, pulled her knickers to one side and licked her until she came in his face, then slid into her hard from behind and fucked her until she climaxed once more, pulling her hair back hard all the while. She loved the contrast between his gentlemanly behaviour in public and his Neanderthal moves when they were alone. When she'd pulled the condom from him and licked his cock clean, he'd groaned, 'God, you're slutty.'

And it clearly wasn't a bad thing, if the speed of his recovery was anything to go by. She suspected that she was bringing out his wild side without even trying – he liked her enough to do whatever she asked. And she liked the way that made her feel.

The next date was a cinema trip with Katie sucking Alex's cock in the back row until he came down her throat, fingers gripping into her shoulders so hard that they left bruises. After that was a Chinese meal, followed by a fuck in a grubby back-alley, giggling as they almost got discovered by a cyclist taking a short-cut; a day at the zoo followed by urgent sex pinned up against the wall the second they got home; and a quiet night in that turned X-rated when Katie produced a hardcore porn film and suggested they tried out some of the action.

Striptease classes took on a whole new meaning for Katie now that she had someone to practice her moves on. After her first night of passion with Alex, Katie had thought she'd have a hard time keeping up: her muscles were also aching in blissful memory. But somehow, the thought of performing for him had spurred her on. Sophie had even commented that watching Katie made her blush, so explicit were her movements. But when Sophie tried to dig further, Katie was closed-mouthed. For some reason, she didn't want to share the details of what was going on with Alex – or even admit there was anything going on at all. It was too personal – and she didn't want to jinx things. She'd already asked Alex to keep what was going on a secret from Sophie, excusing it to him by saying she didn't want to put any pressure on them in the early days.

When Amber propositioned her after class, Katie found herself pretending she was on and not in the mood. Somehow it would have felt wrong to make out with Amber – and while she'd enjoyed the night with her and Tawny, she was nervous about it becoming a regular thing. Although she batted away any romantic thoughts about Alex that crossed her mind, when she went to sleep it was as often to thoughts of Alex holding her and nuzzling her neck as to bending her over and taking her roughly from behind.

Aside from Monday nights, Katie barely had time to stay in touch with Sophie, let alone anyone else. Her daily phone calls to Sophie were replaced with calls to Alex: no matter how long they talked for, they always seemed to have more to say to each other. Luckily Sophie seemed to be in her own little world too, so Katie didn't feel like a bad friend. It was only when Alex mentioned that Sophie had nearly finished her painting that she realised she'd been seeing him for nearly a month. And, she realised with dread, that meant it was time to claim her prize from Ved.

🐌

If Katie was honest with herself, she didn't want to win any more. The last few weeks had been the most fun she'd had in an age. Sure, the sex was dirty but it was more than that: great conversation, lots of laughter and, she was beginning to realise, a fair bit of affection too. She loved the way that Alex kissed the centre of her forehead after sex; snuck his hand into hers when they were watching TV together; reached his foot out under the table to touch hers if they were out in a group, as if to remind her that he was still there for her. And even thinking about curling up with her hand playing in his chest hair made her smile.

Nonetheless, a bet was a bet, and if she didn't claim her prize, Ved would demand his instead. It wasn't as if it was cheating: Alex hadn't actually mentioned monogamy to her yet, although he did seem to spend an awful lot of time looking deep into her eyes, and she'd often got the impression that he wanted to say something to her. But no, she brushed the thought aside. They hadn't agreed on monogamy so she wasn't cheating on him by claiming her prize. And anyway, she didn't have to fuck Ved. It'd be more of a punishment for him if she didn't. On the other hand, if she didn't prove that she'd won, she was certain Ved would make her fuck him, and a whole lot more besides.

The only problem was getting proof that she'd won. She couldn't exactly show Ved how kinky Alex was, although she was sure he'd be very happy to hide in her wardrobe. She guessed she could record a sex session with her webcam, but the idea of Ved watching her and Alex fuck made her feel queasy for some reason. Then it came to her: a phone message. All she had to do was set her mobile phone to record and she could get Alex talking dirty. Once Ved heard some of the things they said to each other he'd know that he'd lost. She sent Alex a text.

'Feeling frisky thinking about you. Good time to call? x'

He texted back instantly. 'Give me 5 mins, honey. Sophie here so will have to go to my room... x'

Five minutes later, Katie was sitting on her own bed, naked but for her silk robe. 'Well, no reason I can't get off at the same time,' she thought. She started to warm herself up with her rabbit so that she'd sound suitably turned on when she spoke to Alex – although to be honest, his deep voice was usually enough to get her wet, particularly when he was reminding her about the experiences they'd already shared. When she knew she was close to coming, she turned the toy off and picked up the phone, pressing the 'record' button on it before she dialled. A momentary pang of guilt struck her, but she knew that she was doing this for the greater good.

'Hi gorgeous. What you up to?'

'Sitting here with a boner waiting for you to call. I

can't believe what you do to me. The second I got your text he was up and ready. Why aren't you here?'

'Because I'm here. Anyway, we agreed that we needed a night off from each other.'

'Yes, and it made sense at the time but I can't for the life of me think why we thought it was a good idea now. Can't you come over?'

'No. One of us has to be strong. But that doesn't mean we can't make each other come.'

'Christ, you're insatiable. What did I do to deserve you?'

'Very good things. Or very bad things. I can't believe I thought you were so straight when we first met.'

'Well, I am straight. I just love fucking you.'

'Oh come on, there's no need to be scared that Sophie will overhear. I know what a filthy bastard you are. You're just as deviant as I am.'

'You're not deviant, Katie. You just love sex.'

'I love *wild* sex. I mean, what's the point if it's just boring sucking and fucking?'

'Do you really think that?' Alex's voice was tense.

'Well, of course. Don't you?'

'You mean the last few weeks have been boring for you?'

'No, not at all. They've been great but then again, you've been a kinky sod.'

'So it's just a sex thing for you?'

Things weren't going the way Katie had planned. Alex was sounding increasingly pissed off by the second.

'Of course it's not just sex. But if we'd just been having dull sex in the missionary position it wouldn't have been the same. I love how experimental you're up for being with me. Remember that night after the Chinese – the expression on that guy's face when he cycled past?'

Katie was trying to bring Alex back on track to salacious thoughts.

'I can remember that you looked so beautiful that I couldn't wait to get you home. I didn't realise it was just some kinky game to you.'

'It wasn't,' Katie said – realising quite how much she was lying as she uttered the words.

'You just said that if it was just dull sex in the missionary position then you'd have dumped me.'

'I *didn't* say that – I was just saying that I'm glad the sex is so good between us and that you're not as uptight as I thought you were. For fuck's sake, get a grip.' By now, Katie was as irritated as Alex and had forgotten the reason for her phone call.

'Me get a grip? I think you're the one who needs to get a grip. I can't believe I thought you were different from the person I first met. It's just about the sex for you, isn't it? It doesn't matter that we can talk until dawn, or that you feel right in my arms, or that you make me laugh. It's just about having some dirty fuck. I don't want to be used like that.'

'You should think yourself lucky – most men would be grateful.' Katie almost spat the words down the phone. She couldn't believe that he hadn't been prepared to compromise for her after all. He was just making her do whatever he wanted, just like Stuart.

'Well, I'm not most men, am I? If all you want is to get fucked then go back to your silly little friends with their stupid outfits and their psychological hang-ups. I'm not just a piece of meat, Katie. I thought you liked me.'

'I do like you…' But as she spoke the words, Katie heard a click. He'd hung up on her. She slammed the phone down hard.

'Wanker!'

Katie felt the tears starting to roll over her cheeks and ran to the bathroom to get some tissues. How dare he make her feel like this? Well, if he thought that all she wanted was sex, she'd prove him right. She took a deep breath, washed her face and poured a large glass of wine. Picking up the phone, she dialled a familiar number.

'Ved. Good news, for you at least. You've won. Fancy claiming your prize tonight?'

Although there were technically a few days left for her to win, there was no way she was ever going to see Alex again, let alone fuck him. She may as well let Ved do his worst.

❧

Katie slipped on the blindfold and knocked on the black door three times, as instructed. She hoped she'd got the right place – she'd never been there before but Ved had been insistent that she met him at a new location. 'You know my place too well. I want somewhere with the element of surprise.'

If she'd got it wrong, the person that opened the door was going to get a shock. Other than the blindfold, she was wearing nothing but a lightweight summer coat and a pair of crippling high heels. As soon as the door opened, she was to remove the coat to reveal her freshly shaved pussy, with the words 'use me' scrawled over her pubic mound in lipstick. Ved was nothing if not creative.

After what seemed like an age, Katie heard the creak of the door and dropped her coat to the floor. She could feel a blush rising on her cheeks. She had no idea who was looking at her – and as a cold hand grabbed her by the wrist and pulled her through the door, she was unable to make any guesses. The only part of the person she could feel was the hand, and she couldn't ascertain whether it was male or female. Katie could smell some unisex cologne and, she thought, a touch of leather. She stumbled as she was led down stairs and was rewarded with a stinging slap to her cheek. Although she trusted Ved implicitly, her adrenaline was still curdling as she reached the bottom of the stairs and heard a solid 'click' as a door was pulled fast behind her.

She could hear a babble of voices and smell smoke and sweat in the air. What *was* this place? A sex club? A home? An illegal bar? Was she being paraded in front of perverts or exposing herself in front of a room full of shocked strangers? Even though she was genuinely scared, she could also feel her cunt moistening at the infinite possibilities. She knew that Ved would take advantage of his win to push her further than she'd ever gone before.

She felt her hands being tethered behind her back with some kind of coarse rope that chafed her wrists, then pulled up uncomfortably behind her head. There was more fumbling and she realised, as she was tugged forward, that someone had tied a second rope between her wrists to use as a lead. She stumbled again, and noticed the sound dying down as she was pushed downwards from her shoulders and felt a chair underneath her arse. The second rope was knotted behind her, securing her to the chair, arms still raised. She could already feel the lactic acid build up, but that was nothing compared to being unable to move her hands to protect her modesty.

Just as Katie thought it was over – or about to start – her legs were forced widely apart and she felt cool metal against them – a solid spreader bar, at least four feet across, that would ensure she couldn't close her legs at any point. Strong hands lifted her up in the chair, repositioning her so that she was perched on the edge of it, leaning back slightly, with both arse and cunt exposed. Her breathing was rapid now, and as she felt the cool fingers slip inside her, coated with a cold slippery substance, she couldn't help herself from moaning with shock. Another slap around her face reminded her that she had to stay silent.

She felt more fingers probing her holes – the same ones or others, she wasn't quite sure. There was a bright flash of pain as she felt something being attached to her labia – a clip on each side – and pulled tightly out to open her out fully. The pain was bearable but the lack of knowledge about what was going on was making her heart thump. Who could see her? Who could touch her? She knew she'd agreed to no safe word but now she was beginning to wonder if she'd made the right call.

Just as she was beginning to panic, she heard a reassuring whisper in her ear.

'Good to see you, sweetheart. Every last inch of you too. I do like a girl who follows orders. So do you want to know where you are?'

'Yes,' Katie gasped in relief.

'I thought you would. Oh well. Maybe later. Now, let's see how that cunt's bearing up.'

Ved's familiar fingers played around her lubed entrance, then slid inside her, first pussy, then arse, two fingers in each, splaying out as if to give himself a better view. Katie breathed in, trying to control her moans. Ved knew her body so well that he could take her to the edge of orgasm with little more than a single touch – and cool her down just as quickly. Which he did now, administering a harsh flick of his finger and thumb to her clit.

'The rules are simple, my dear. You're mine for the night. No safe words, no limits. After that, you are free to go. Is that understood?'

'Yes.'

'Yes, Master. You're my slave, not my friend now.' There was a chilling tone to Ved's voice. Katie had heard it before and knew it was just part of his play but nonetheless felt a thrill of fear.

'Yes, Master.'

'Well, first of all, I think we'll put that tongue to use.'

Katie felt Ved's cock pressing against her lips and opened her mouth obediently. He pressed his cock forwards until he was pushing against her tonsils. She felt the gag start to rise and controlled it by swallowing.

'Good girl,' he said, then began to thrust back and forth. 'I'm just going to use your mouth as my fuckhole.

And then my friends are going to do the same. I know what an oral fixation you've got, you little slut. May as well take advantage of it.'

Katie could do nothing to control his movements. Her head moved back and forth as he thrust into her, her body moving to his rhythm.

'Open your mouth wider, slut,' he ordered and she did as she was told.

'That's it. I want to see that pretty pink tongue of yours. And cover it with my cum.'

Katie felt Ved's movements speeding and soon her mouth was filling up with his salty load.

'Ah, that's better,' he said. 'Now that I've used that darling little mouth of yours to despunk, I think I should introduce you to one of my friends. Meet Simon.'

It was quite an introduction. Katie felt another cock being pushed into her mouth, this one thicker than Ved's, if slightly shorter. Hands tangled in her hair as the owner crudely fucked her mouth, this time pulling out to spray his load all over her face.

'Pretty as a picture,' she heard Ved laugh. 'Who's next? You're going to be a busy girl tonight, darling – you should make a lot of new friends.'

Katie's imagination ran away with her: was there a queue of men, cocks out, all watching her humiliation? Or was Ved just playing with her mind? For all she knew, he could be lying about the audience – perhaps it was just him and a mate taking it in turns? Or maybe it wasn't strangers, but instead all the people he'd watched her fuck at Decadence over the years? Anyone could be there and, under the terms of the bet, anything could happen. It was sex in its rawest form. She was nothing but a body to fuck and be fucked by: the idea turned her on. As another cock pushed its way into her mouth, stretching her lips wide with its girth, she focussed her attention on sucking it to the best of her ability. A bet is a bet, after all, and she wanted to make sure that Ved had no cause for complaint.

An hour later, Katie had lost track of the amount of cock she'd sucked. Some of the guys had made her swallow, forcing their cocks against her tonsils so she didn't spill a single drop. Others had spunked over her face, her tits, her neck. Her hair was tangled from the many hands that had pulled at it. Her nipples were hard from the guys who'd pinched them, licked them, bitten them, taken her breasts roughly in their hands and squeezed her pert breasts together to use for a tit-wank. She knew that her pussy was dripping, even though the only physical stimulation she'd had below the waist was from the cruel clamps stretching her wide.

Ved had played her perfectly: she'd told him enough times that sucking cock turned her on and he'd given her more cock than she'd ever had in one night before. But now her jaw was starting to ache, and her hands were beginning to get pins and needles from being restricted for so long. She felt someone holding them, rubbing them firmly to restore the blood flow, then untying the bonds from her arms. A glass was placed in her hand.

'Gargle with this,' Ved said.

She did as she was told, tasting a minty slightly alcoholic substance, and then 'spit'. Her head was pulled over, she guessed to aim at a bowl.

'Just mouthwash, dear, nothing to be scared of. Needed to get your mouth nice and clean for round two.'

Katie felt the clips being removed from her labia and legs being untied from the spreader bar before being instructed to walk around. Again, she wobbled, having forgotten about the heels she was wearing thanks to her previous hour's oral escapades. Still blindfolded, she was led to a bed and laid flat on her back. She felt a scraping over her body that she couldn't identify, then a warm flannel run all over her, cleaning her up, while Ved gave her an affectionate kiss. Maybe he was going to go gently on her after all. She hungrily returned the kiss, desperate to be fucked, but all too soon Ved pulled away.

'After all that cock, I thought you might be getting a little jaded,' he said, and Katie felt a pair of thighs straddling her face. 'So here's some pussy instead. I know what a little dyke you are.'

He knew how much Katie hated the word, which was exactly why he used it. Katie's mouth was filled with the taste of wet pussy, and she began sucking on the stranger's clit, flickering her tongue over it, enjoying the power kick as she felt it stiffen in her mouth. This was hardly punishment, but she guessed she deserved a break after her obedient cock-sucking.

'Faster,' the stranger moaned, as she ground her quim all over Katie's lips. Katie did as requested, but it clearly wasn't enough for the woman she was tending to, who started rocking herself back and forth against Katie's lips and nose, pressing her wetness hard into her face. All Katie could smell was pussy and all she could taste was the woman's musky juice. Her own clit, meanwhile, was woefully unattended.

'Oh, and Ella's brought her boyfriend with her to give you a helping hand.'

At first, Katie didn't realise what Ved meant, and when she felt the bed move with the pressure of another body, she thought that she was going to get some relief at the new addition's hand – or better yet, cock. Instead, Ella, as she now knew the woman grinding on her face to be called, lifted up briefly, removing her clit from Katie's mouth. Katie heard her moan, and then the pussy was pressed into her face once more, but something was different. The angle had changed and, as Katie resumed licking, she realised there was a new sharper taste mingling with Ella's juices. It couldn't be... fuck...there was suddenly no mistaking it. Ella was being fucked from behind while Katie licked her clit.

'Open your mouth,' a deep male voice ordered her and Katie did as instructed. A cock was thrust right to the back of her throat, wet with juices, then pulled out just as abruptly. Katie realised that he was alternating thrusts between Ella's pussy and her own mouth. She was being used by a man and a woman at the same time: an idea that made her cunt flood. Just how filthy was Ved going to make her be?

'Smile,' she heard Ved say, and there was an unmistakable 'click'.

'I thought you might like a souvenir so I'm making you a little photo album,' Ved said. 'Of course, if you don't do exactly as you're told then I might just keep it for myself. Or perhaps put it on the internet so that everyone can see exactly what a depraved slut you are. You have no idea how good you looked covered in cum earlier.'

'Bastard!' Katie thought. She'd told him once that her ultimate fantasy — and ultimate fear — was of finding graphic pictures of herself on the internet. Even though she loved experiencing every debauchery available, she hated the idea of some anonymous guy wanking over images of her. But in some dark part of her mind, she also felt intensely aroused at the idea of being splayed open for anyone to get off on.

The couple continued using her mouth, the guy's cock sliding ever-deeper into her throat. Then, just as Katie was getting into the rhythm, he stopped and she felt Ella moving faster over her face as her boyfriend started to fuck her hard. The orgasmic cadenza rose as the pair came closer and closer to orgasm, then 'Aaaaah', the guy screamed out, and Katie felt her mouth being filled with a mixture of his spunk and Ella's juices. The pair stayed in position for a while, catching their breath, then Katie heard Ved's voice once more.

'Ella, darling, can you pull up a bit and spread your lips wide. I want to get a picture of that cum dripping from your pussy into Katie's mouth.'

Katie was shocked at how much the image turned her on, and opened her mouth wide, sticking out her tongue to give the best possible image. After all, she was blindfolded so there was no way she'd be identifiable, even if Ved did release the pics. And perhaps he'd let her come if she showed she was willing to comply with even his most deviant wishes.

Five hours later, she was still dreaming of getting some physical respite. Ved had worked his way through every dark fantasy she'd ever mentioned to him: being fucked by two guys in the pussy at the same time; sucking cock while being spanked; being forced to go down on a row of women, getting them turned on enough for Ved to fuck them. All the while, he'd left the blindfold on, so she could only work out what was happening from the sound effects: the wet slappings, orgasmic groans, dirty talk bursting from people's lips; and from the used pussies and cocks pushed into her mouth to lick clean. And all the while, Ved had banned her from coming.

'You're here for my pleasure, not your own,' he'd said cruelly, as he'd watched her being fucked by the two men. 'Don't even think about coming or your night's going to get a lot longer. Still, only five hours to go.'

'Can I go to the loo?' Katie asked. Over the course of the night, Ved had been feeding her champagne and the pressure on her bladder was beginning to get uncomfortable.

'You don't get any breaks, sweetheart. If you need to piss you can do it right here with all of us watching.'

Katie had never dabbled with watersports and the idea of pissing in public was too shaming.

'Please?' she begged, but Ved was insistent.

'You do as I say. That's what we agreed.' Ved was using his dirty-talk tone, and Katie knew that whatever she said, he wouldn't budge from his decision. Despite her discomfort, the idea turned her on.

Katie knew that her clit was obviously swollen, and

her juices were running down her thighs after all the attention she'd been getting. So when Ved then told her that he was going to punish her for any arousal at all, she knew she was in trouble. For the first time in the evening, he ran his fingers between her cunt lips.

'God, you really are a horny little tramp, aren't you?' he said.

Katie nodded.

'Answer me.' There was a distinct air of threat in Ved's voice.

'Yes, Master, I'm a horny little tramp.'

'You're not supposed to be enjoying yourself. I think you need a thrashing to remind you of your place.'

Ved pulled Katie over his knee, and started spanking her, alternating his slaps between each of her cheeks. At first, he was gentle but as Katie wriggled in his lap, he slapped harder until tears were running down Katie's face, half in bliss, half in pain. Her head was spinning as the endorphins raced through her body, and it took her a second to register that he'd stopped.

'On all fours,' he ordered. Katie obeyed, and felt hands on each of her cheeks, spreading her wide.

'Now *that* is a lovely view,' Ved said. 'Don't you agree?'

Katie could hear a mumble of appreciative voices and felt herself blushing once more. It was easy to forget that she wasn't alone with Ved when he got her into such a trance state. She was even wetter now than she had been before and wondered what was going to happen next.

'So, little Katie, are you having fun?' Ved said.

'Yes, Master.'

'Well you're not supposed to be.' And with a loud 'thwack', Katie felt him slap her directly on the cunt. The pain was so intense that she couldn't help but squeal. It didn't do anything to stop Ved, who kept a relentless pace of slaps, to her soft inner thighs, reddened arse cheeks, slippery labia and, worse, directly onto her clit. Katie didn't think she could take much more and was going to cry out the safe word in the hope Ved would pay attention after all, when he caught her once more across the clit and she felt her own juices splashing over her thighs. Even though the pain was intense, it was transferring into a hot glow that made her clit pulse. She stopped noticing the pain and instead relished the sensation of hard pressure on her wet cunt. And as Ved delivered five slaps in rapid succession to her clit, she couldn't control her body any more: she came hard over his hand, ejaculating into his palm and – to her shame – pissing all over him as the orgasm flowed through her body.

'Oh dear, Katie. Now you're in trouble,' Ved said. 'I think you'd better clean that up.'

He wiped his wet hand over her face, forcing his fingers into her mouth for her to lick, then picked her up by the scruff of the neck and pushed her face down, she assumed towards the puddle of piss. She couldn't do it: couldn't degrade herself so much in public. But as she edged nearer, Ved said, 'Don't tell me you're going to bail out again? First Alex, now me.'

Katie gulped, partly in fear, partly to get rid of the tears that were threatening to spill out at the sudden reminder of Alex.

She tentatively stuck her tongue out and Ved pushed her harder, so that her nose and cheeks were wet with her own urine.

'Lick it.'

As she began to lap, she heard another click, and Ved laughing as he invited other people along to watch her in her ultimate moment of shame.

'That's it, nearly got it all,' Ved said, after what seemed like years. But just as she thought she'd be able to stop, he said, 'Of course, as you pissed on me, it's only fair that I get to piss on you. Open wide.'

The spray of piss hit Katie full in the face, soaking her hair and running down her cheeks. As she felt Ved force her mouth open and grip it tightly so that she didn't miss a single drop, she knew that she'd gone as far as it was possible to go. And, despite her utter degradation, she'd be wanking about it for a long time to come.

❧

By the time morning came around, Katie was shattered. She'd been ravaged by more people than she could keep count of; pussies, cocks and arseholes had all been pushed into her face at Ved's order, only being removed when her expert tongue had given the owner sufficient pleasure; she'd been spanked, paddled, cropped, slapped and forced to drink Ved's piss; she'd been displayed in her ruined state, then been hosed off and dressed in a tight corset and collar, and been led around on a lead. And now, she was on all fours being a 'table' for Ved, having to stay absolutely still because he'd balanced a candelabra on her back and every time she moved, hot wax spilled onto her skin. To make things harder for her, Ved was occasionally tapping her red arse with a riding crop, and giggling when she winced at the pain of the lash and the falling wax. But when an alarm went off, he stopped abruptly and removed the candelabra. He took her hand. 'Stand up.'

She did as she was told and was led through to a small room.

'You can take off the blindfold now. It's ten minutes before your time's up but you can get changed before your final challenge.'

Katie did as she was told, and realised that she was in a shower room.

'There's Jo Malone shower gel – that's your favourite, isn't it..?' Katie nodded. '…and shampoo. Body lotion and towels in the corner. A clean set of clothes hanging up behind the door. Get yourself cleaned up and I'll see you out there once you're done. Take as long as you want.'

Katie enjoyed the feeling of the shower playing over her aching muscles. Although she felt proud of herself for not welching on the bet, she knew that she'd broken through every limit she'd ever had in one night. It had been fun, but as time went on, it had begun to feel a bit empty. OK, she was getting to experiment with everything she'd ever dreamed about in her darkest, dirtiest fantasies but now it was done, there was a strange sense of anti-climax, a sort of 'Is that it?' After the first few hours, things had begun to feel samey. Sure, she was experiencing new sensations but there wasn't any connection going on beyond the mere physical. Other than the few moments that Ved had kissed her, she'd felt like she could have been anyone and it wouldn't have mattered to the people playing with her. That had added to the turn-on for her but now she found her mind drifting back to Alex.

When Alex kissed her, there'd been real passion there. When he pulled her hair, he knew it was because she turned him on, not because he liked doing that to all women. When he'd come inside her, it had been Katie he was fucking, not just a random hole. She shook her head and turned the shower up, trying to drown out the unwelcome thoughts, the tears that were threatening to flow. It was just endorphin come-down, she tried to convince herself. Alex was an arrogant bastard who only wanted to have things his way. She wasn't going to waste time on another selfish git like Stuart.

She got out of the shower, dried herself off and slathered aloe vera body lotion over her reddened and bruised skin. It was soothing and, as she saw the clothes that Ved had chosen for her – faded jeans and a snug cashmere jumper, along with comfy trainers – she started to feel better. Maybe Ved would be able to help, if he wasn't already otherwise engaged? She pushed open the door, curious to finally see her night's surroundings.

Katie blinked at the view that met her. It was a deserted club, with Art Deco style furnishings and big mirrors on the walls. At the front was a small stage – she guessed that had been where she'd started off – and to the right was a velvet curtain that was partially open, showing a four-poster bed. The only sign that it had been full of people was the pile of glasses neatly stacked on the bar.

'Thought you'd appreciate having the place to yourself,' Ved said. She started at his voice, and realised he was sitting in a dark corner of the room. 'And this way, no one else will know what you really look like. OK, they might give you a double take if you go into the club but you can always deny it. Oh, by the way…' Ved pulled a camera out of his bag. 'This is the only camera that was used all night.

Here are all the memory sticks. Delete them, look at them, whatever. I want you to know that you're safe.'

Katie smiled.

'Thanks, babe.'

'Meh, play is one thing. I knew it'd get you off on it if you thought you might get caught. Sometimes you're a predictable little trollop. But I didn't want you to be worried afterwards.'

Ved ruffled her hair affectionately as he spoke. 'So, had fun?' he asked.

'Yeah, it was great. Wild,' Katie said.

'No, really, I'm asking you as a friend. Have you had fun?'

Katie paused, thinking.

'Yes, although I'm going to be paying for it for the rest of the week.' She rubbed her aching shoulders, and Ved beckoned her to move closer and turn round so that he could massage her. 'But there was something missing.'

'I tried to do everything I could think of. Other than piercing you, cutting you or bringing a dog in, I can't think of much else we could have done.'

'I don't mean that,' Katie said. 'It just made me realise – well – sometimes sex isn't just about what's happening to your body.'

'Oh fuck. You've fallen, haven't you?'

'No,' Katie snapped. Then… 'why do you say that?'

'I've seen it happen time and time again, sweetheart. Girl breaks up with boy. Girl fucks everyone on the planet. Girl gets kinky. Girl falls in love. Girl goes off kink.'

'It's not that I've gone off kink. It's just…'

'…that you'd rather have been having sex with Alex, without a single paddle in sight, than getting treated like a dirty whore by half of London?'

'Well, errr, yes. Although…' Katie smiled wryly. 'I don't think that's going to happen again. We had a row earlier, and I don't think he'd be too impressed if he heard about tonight. Still, at least I got some material for the wank bank. Better than a kick in the teeth.'

'You silly girl. Why didn't you tell me? And don't be so fatalistic – why do you say it's not going to happen again with Alex? It was only one row. Maybe if you give him a call you can sort it out. No one but us needs know about tonight. It's not like anyone else will recognise you. Why do you think I kept you blindfolded all night?'

'Bless you. But Alex is so vanilla, though. It would never work. He's just like Stuart.'

'How?'

'What do you mean, how? I've told you. He's vanilla. Only into sucking and fucking.'

'And do you enjoy it?'

'Well, yes.'

'And do you get it enough?'

'Yes.'

'And did you get it enough with Stuart?'

'Christ, no.'

'And is there any way, other than the fact that he doesn't like Decadence, that Alex in any way resembles Stuart?'

'Err, well, he makes me laugh like Stuart did. More, actually.'

'The bastard! How could you possibly go out with someone that makes you laugh. Anything else?'

'No, but he was just so insistent that he wasn't into kink and he knows how important it is to me. If he loved me then surely he'd be up for doing whatever I asked.'

'Doesn't that go both ways?'

As Ved looked at her, his kind eyes not flinching away from her angry gaze, Katie knew what she had to do.

'Anyway, enough of this talk. Here's the last bit of your challenge.'

Ved pushed a champagne glass towards Katie. 'Over the night I've been collecting the cum sparked over your body – and a selection of other fluids. Drink this and you're free to go.'

Katie was momentarily appalled, then looked Ved straight in the eye and raised the glass up in a toast.

'To pushing the limits,' she said.

Ved tapped his glass of champagne against her glass.

'To love.'

CHAPTER SIX

Endgame

'So are you sure he'll speak to me?' Katie asked Sophie for the tenth time. She'd filled her in on almost all the background the day after the 'punishment', omitting to mention the bet and her subsequent sordid night. Sophie was hoping for a reconciliation almost as much as Katie was, now she'd been convinced of Katie's change of heart. 'I told you, I don't know but I can't see him making a scene at my launch. And you'd better promise me that you won't either. I don't want to have to worry about that on top of everything else.'

Sophie's celebrity client had decided that he'd present his girlfriend with the picture at a private viewing. He'd hired an exclusive Knightbridge gallery for the night, and paid them to remove their current exhibition and replace all their artwork with Sophie's paintings. In the final room, Sophie's picture of the girlfriend would be in pride of place, hidden behind a pair of curtains that the star would open with a flourish.

Katie had to admit that the star had charm. She couldn't think of many men that would go to that much effort for a girlfriend's birthday, particularly not for such an obvious tabloid tart as Celia Chah. When the star had first told

Sophie his plans, she called Katie, freaked out that she hadn't got enough work to fill the walls, but after a few phone calls to her parents, who'd got some of her old degree show work in storage, and to friends she'd given paintings for their birthdays, along with working late into the night on some new work, Sophie had just about got enough together. Her client was doing all the planning for the party – or rather, she suspected, his PA was – and had insisted that Sophie come along so that she could see the look on his girlfriend's face when she got the painting. He'd foisted a bundle of tickets into her hands for her friends, 'so that you don't get bored talking to all the acting types. They're so self-obsessed but Celia loves them and what Celia wants…' He'd raised his eyebrows and Sophie had giggled.

Normally, Katie would have been excited at the idea of going to a celeb-filled party but her worries about seeing Alex were overriding all else. She'd thought about calling him but she was scared he'd hang up on her again and didn't want to take the risk. She could just about cope with being hung up on once but if he did it again, she'd never have the guts to try again.

When Sophie had mentioned the party, she knew that it was the perfect opportunity. There was no way that Alex would miss out on Sophie's big night, and it would make sense that she'd be there too. She just hoped that she could think of the right thing to say. No matter how many times she went over it in her head, she could hear the hurt in Alex's voice as he said 'it's just about some dirty fuck'. Looking back on their phone conversation, she was hardly surprised that he'd hung up on her. She must have sounded like a heartless bitch.

❧

Katie anxiously dug her thumb against the corners of the thick card invitation that was her passport to Alex. She'd had to give up on applying eyeliner because her hands were shaking so much, and had changed outfits four times before she eventually settled on a simple black trouser suit with a dark green chiffon camisole top and strappy heels. It was sexy but subtly so: she didn't want to wear anything too slutty in case Alex thought that she was trying to seduce him – even though she was – or, worse, was trying to pull one of the celebs.

When she walked in, past the huge bouncer who nodded her through after carefully checking her invitation, Katie ignored the glittering crowd of celebs and media types. She barely glanced at the waiters carrying trays of canapés: quails breast with pear jelly cubes; egg shells full of scrambled egg with caviar and white truffle; shot glasses of lobster bisque with langoustine foam; and griddled asparagus spears tied with chives and drizzled with hollandaise. She accepted the glass of champagne that was pressed into her hand by a pretty waitress dressed in a metallic shift dress, but the smile she gave her in thanks didn't reach her eyes, which were already drifting off to see if she could find her quarry.

The gallery was on the top floor of a regency-style house, with floor to ceiling windows that offered spectacular views of London. Rather than the usual minimalist style that galleries tend to adopt, it was designed to be comfortably kitsch, with elegant chaise longues, battered leather sofas and mismatched but somehow complementary antique chairs. The doorways were flanked by display cabinets filled with quirky objects d'art – a Victorian glass case of mice playing violins, a bunch of flowers spun out of brightly coloured glass, a bemused-looking battered teddy bear. And Sophie's art was on every wall.

Katie moved through the room, head turning from left to right, trying not to make it too obvious that she was looking for someone, smiling as she caught sight of the occasional familiar piece of Sophie's work. But although there was only a smattering of people, she couldn't see Alex anywhere. The next room was more crowded and still she had no joy. She saw Sophie and went over to her to congratulate her with a hug.

'Well done. Your paintings look fab – just as I

expected. How does it feel?'

'Terrifying,' Sophie said. 'People keep on coming up to me and asking about my work. It feels so weird chatting about it while I'm trying not to blurt out "That film you were in last summer was ace". I feel like an imposter.'

'Don't be daft,' Katie said. 'You've worked your arse off to get here. Just enjoy it. You're looking gorgeous by the way.'

'Oh, this,' Sophie joked, having clearly blown most of her commission on the white beaded dress that hugged her curvy form. 'Well, you know, got to make an effort.'

'Is Jake coming then? Or are you on the pull?'

'Ah, Jake. I forgot that you didn't know.'

'What?'

'Well, he is coming…'

'But…'

'So's his boyfriend. Turns out there was a reason he was so gentlemanly. Bit embarrassing when he told me just as I was going to go for a snog after what I thought was our first date. He was only being so friendly because, err, he likes me.'

'Gah! Sorry about that. You know my gaydar sucks. You OK?'

'I'm fine,' Sophie said. 'Plenty more fish in the sea and all that. I mean, just look around.'

Katie followed Sophie's expansive hand gesture and

could see why she had no complaints about being single tonight. The room did seem particularly full of tasty specimens, half of whom were famous. It was prime flirting ground, even if she was surprised that Sophie saw it as such. Katie was even more surprised to realise that *she* didn't care.

'True. Err, so, is Alex here?'

'Yes, he helped me set up. He was somewhere over there the last time I saw him.' Sophie pointed towards a door in the corner of the room. 'Maybe he's gone outside to have a smoke?'

'That's a good idea,' Katie said. 'You OK if I leave you to it?'

'Like I could stop you. Good luck,' Sophie said. 'Make sure you're back in here at nine, though. That's when they're unveiling the painting. I hope she likes it. In the meantime, I think I'm going to get a cocktail from the bar. So many cute guys to talk to there.'

Katie wondered at Sophie's confidence. She seemed so much more vibrant than usual. The old Sophie would have sat in a corner blushing. She'd have to find out what had happened in the last month to effect such a change. But first things first... She headed for the door in the corner and pushed it open.

When she stepped outside, Katie couldn't hold back her gasp. She was standing on an expansive roof terrace.

Ivy-covered trellis on all sides of the roof meant that she couldn't see the cityscape below, and the roof was high enough up that there was no ambient street noise so it felt like she was in the middle of the countryside. Gravel pathways led to different walled areas and, as Katie started wandering, she realised each one was differently themed. There was a Bedouin tent at the end of one pathway, with people spilling out clutching cups of mint tea, and hookahs set up for anyone to enjoy. The next space was a fairytale daydream of twinkling lights, strange-looking giant mushrooms and oversized daisies. She was sure that she could smell someone having a spliff. She walked past a pond full of flamingos with a bridge over it leading to a pagoda serving Chinese take-outs in black lacquer boxes; a bustling barbecue area with a chef serving fresh steaks, garlic-stuffed lamb and chicken satay; and a picnic area complete with miniature hampers of game pie, Scotch eggs, chicken drumsticks, poached salmon and hunks of organic bread, and waiters circulating with jugs of Pimms. Still no Alex.

Katie turned down yet another pathway, wondering just how big the roof terrace was, and found herself in a monastic-style garden with arches on all sides. It felt peaceful, with no entertainment going on other than a string quartet playing in the corner, and just a few candles for light. It took her eyes a few moments to adjust to the dimness but when they did, she noticed that the area was almost deserted. A kissing couple sat on one bench, so immersed in their passion that she could have stood right next to them and they wouldn't have noticed her. And on the opposite bench sat a lone figure: Alex. He seemed lost in his own thoughts and Katie deliberately kept her footfall light as she walked over to him, for fear of scaring him away.

'Hello you,' she said.

Alex started.

'Oh, err, hi. What are you doing here?'

'Well, it is my best mate's big launch. I couldn't really miss it.'

'Yeah, but why aren't you in there with all the party people? Would have thought that was more your pace.'

'I was looking for you.'

'Oh.'

Katie bit the inside of her lip, wondering what to say next. She decided honesty was the best policy.

'Look, I'm sorry about the other night. I was fucked up. I didn't know what I wanted and I took it out on you. My ex – well, he wasn't into sex. I was blaming you for stuff that he did. He kept on turning me down no matter what I did. I tried asking for it, not asking for it, dressing up. I even had a threesome with him because he said it would turn him on. All that happened was that he fucked the other girl and ignored me. I felt like the ugliest woman in the planet when we split up. It took me six months to realise that anyone might actually want to have sex with me and I guess I've been making up for it ever since. I thought you were going the same way as he was and it freaked me out.'

Katie stopped abruptly. That was more than enough honesty. She was admitting things that she'd only really admitted to herself in the last few days. And she trusted Ved to keep her secret about the sordid night that had changed so much so there was no need to burden Alex with it.

Alex laughed. Katie looked at him, shocked.

'What's so funny?'

'You,' he said, pulling her to him and kissing her hard. 'I can't believe you've been such an idiot. We've been such idiots. Wanna know why I hate the kink scene so much?'

'Go on…'

'When I was in New York, I was with this girl Angela for a couple of years. When we first met the sex was great but as time went on, she got more and more experimental. I didn't mind at first – what bloke's going to turn down the chance to have a threesome with two women, or shag his girlfriend up the arse? But then she wanted to get into more extremes. She asked me to choke her during sex, and cut her. When I told her I wasn't comfortable with that, she said we should go open. I hated the idea of it but since I couldn't give her what she wanted, I thought it was only fair.'

'That's well out of order!' Katie said.

'And I was well in love,' Alex replied. 'Anyway, she started seeing this professional Dom guy and she'd come back covered in bruises but grinning from ear to ear. After a while, things started to get more heavy: he'd ban her from having sex with me for a week, or order her to go out late at night wearing a short skirt and no knickers into really dangerous areas. I was worried about her and told her so but she just said that I didn't get it. In the end, she left me for him. I guess I should have seen it coming. When you started telling me our sex life was boring, it was as if I was speaking to Angela all over again. I guess I flipped out.'

'I didn't say our sex life was boring,' Katie said. 'Come on, you know how hard I was coming for you.'

'I wasn't thinking straight. All I could hear when you started having a go was Angela taunting me for being a little straight boy.'

'Well, you should know the sex we had was amazing,' Katie said, running her hand up his thigh. 'Sure, I like the kinky stuff but given the choice between the wildest night ever with a load of deviant strangers, or a night with you, I know which one I'd choose.'

'Are you sure?'

Katie thought back to her night with Ved, a smile playing across her lips.

'I'm certain. I don't need any of that stuff. There are more important things.'

Alex leaned forward and stroked Katie's cheek.

'I can't believe what an arse I've been. Sorry.'

'I'm the one who should be apologising,' Katie said, reaching up to stroke his neck.

The pair looked at each other, fingers delicately tracing each other's cheekbones, playing softly around each other's hairlines, running over each other's lips as if seeing each other for the first time. It was impossible to tell who moved first, but suddenly their lips were touching. Katie's lips yielded to Alex's, as he pecked her lower lip, pushed his full lips against hers, then slowly deepened the kiss, sucking her lower lip between his and running his tongue over it. Katie moaned, her tongue moving to meet his, unable to stop herself from softly biting his lower lip in response. Her hands trailed over his neck, his over her waist. They both lost themselves in the kiss, moving ever-closer, hands gripping ever-tighter, lips pressing ever-harder, until the sound of fireworks dragged them back into reality and Katie pulled away.

'Fuck!' she said, looking Alex right in the eye.

'My thoughts entirely,' he said. 'How come we haven't

spent more time doing that?'

'Because if we did, there's a very real chance I'd pass out. My head's swimming,' Katie said.

'That's just the champagne,' Alex said, but the squeeze that he gave her hand showed Katie that he felt the same way. 'So, shall we head inside?'

Katie looked at her watch. '8.45 – yep, we'd better. They'll be doing the big unveiling soon.'

❧

'Happy birthday, darling,' the actor said. 'This is for you – a Sophie Masters' original.'

He pulled the cord to open the curtains and there was an appreciative murmur throughout the crowd. Sophie had captured his girlfriend perfectly, from her cute snub nose to her long golden hair, the way that she stood with her hip jutting out in a 'look at me' pose, to the naughty sparkle of her eyes. One person started clapping and soon the gallery was buzzing with the noise of a roomful of people showing their appreciation with claps and whoops. There was only one person who didn't look impressed: Celia.

'I told you I wanted a car. I can't believe you got me this piece of shit. What do I need a painting for? I *know* what I look like.'

The spikey blonde turned on her heel and stormed down the stairs, leaving an embarrassed and open-mouthed crowd. Sophie burst into tears and raced into the gardens, with Katie and Alex following rapidly behind her. After a moment's silence, the crowd started babbling once more and ten minutes later, it was as if everyone had forgotten there had been any scene at all. There was food, drink and conversation: what more did they need?

❧

'Well, that was different!' Katie said to Alex, as they lay curled up in his bed.

'Certainly was. Still, all's well that ends well. Sophie seemed happy enough by the end of the night.' He squeezed her arm affectionately and leaned over to peck her on the lips.

'I don't think the night's quite ended yet,' Katie said, putting her arm around him and running her nails softly up and down his back, circling at the base of his spine. She felt his cock stiffen against her thigh and pressed her body closer to his, tilting her face for him to kiss her. 'Tonight, it's your rules,' she said. 'I don't need you to scratch me or bite me or talk dirty to me. I don't need to be your whore or have you come over my face. However you want to play is fine by me.'

'I'm not playing anything, Katie. This isn't a game,' Alex said, and pulled her on top of him, straddling his hardness, then moved up to kiss her. Katie kissed him back hungrily, rubbing her clit against the base of his cock so that he could feel she was already wet for him. He ground back against her briefly, then reached down to pull a condom out of his jeans pocket.

Slipping it on, he flipped Katie onto her back and began to trace his cock over her clit, rubbing up and down and side to side, teasing her by putting it at her entrance then, just as she thought he was going to thrust inside her, pulling away to rub it over her clit once more. All the while he was kissing her, stroking her hair, rubbing her arms and scratching her neck. Katie kept arching up towards him but he put his hands on her hips, holding her in place until eventually, he could take it no more and slid inside her yielding cunt.

Katie gasped as she felt him enter her. She'd forgotten how perfectly he fitted her body, and she instinctively arched her back and grabbed his arse to pull him deeper inside her.

'Open your eyes and look at me,' Alex said.

Katie hesitated for a second, then did as she'd been asked, shocked to see the emotion in Alex's face.

'Keep looking at me as you come,' Alex said, and began to thrust slowly and steadily, cock grinding against her clit at every thrust, hands moving to her nipples to play with them as he fucked her. Katie could feel her orgasm building up and struggled to match Alex's gaze, forcing herself to keep her eyes open despite the pleasure. As Alex sped up and thrust particularly deeply into her, Katie felt herself release and looked Alex right in the eyes as wave after wave of orgasm crashed through her. He followed suit seconds later, gazing at her equally intently as he came, forehead scrunched in a frown with the pressure but eyes liquid with genuine affection. As the last spasms of orgasm pulsed through her body, Katie felt tears start to run down her cheeks in raw emotion.

'Are you OK?' Alex asked, worried.

'Perfect. Just perfect,' she said, reaching up to pull him into another kiss. As the pair of them drifted off to sleep, she knew it was the best orgasm she'd had in years.

❧

It was quite some crowd that walked into Decadence the following weekend. Katie led the way, in a high-necked full-length clingy black lycra dress that was slashed to the thigh and laced up the front. Behind her, with his hand on her arse, was Alex. He'd gone for a more sedate look: tight black jeans, boots and a flouncy white shirt. Sophie was next in line, wearing a purple corset with gold trim, flouncy three-quarter-length net skirt and can-can boots in matching colours; and she was holding the hand of a well-muscled man wearing tight leather jeans, a black shirt and a leather gimp hood. Ved led the rear in a red zoot suit over bare chest, with a beaming Lucy on one arm, dressed in a little black dress with visible stockings and suspenders, and Amber on the other in a silver glittery bikini and shimmering marabou stole. The mood was high as the group walked over to the most exclusive of the booths to find it already sporting three buckets of champagne.

'Just let me know if you want to leave at any point, gorgeous,' Katie whispered in Alex's ear. He smiled at her.

'I dunno, I can see there might be benefits in coming here.' He gestured at the pair of bunny girls walking over to their table holding trays full of vodka jelly.

'Oi, you.' Katie playfully smacked Alex on the arm. 'You're taken.'

'And I wouldn't have it any other way.' Alex kissed the end of Katie's nose.

'At it already? Honestly, some people just don't know how to behave in public,' Ved joked, simultaneously sliding his hand up Amber's thigh and slipping a finger inside her bikini bottoms. She slapped his hand away.

'I told you, you first. You want to get inside me, I get to get inside you. For as long as I want.'

Katie had discovered, after the third striptease class,

that Amber wasn't a radical lesbian. She played Domme with men and only had relationships with women. From that point, Katie had sworn to herself that she had to get her and Ved together: Amber was the only person she thought might be able to tame him, which was something she was desperate to see. OK, her punishment had been fun but she still wanted to get one up on Ved. And sure enough, at Amber's hand Ved looked chastened – something Katie had never seen before. As Amber moved her hand up to cruelly pull his pierced nipple, and he groaned, Katie thought that Ved may finally have met his match.

Lucy was looking shocked at the people filling Decadance: a man in a straightjacket and woman on a collar and lead with a puppy tail butt plug, both being led around by a black-cloaked thigh-booted Domme; a woman naked but for body paint; a woman with perfect breasts – and an obvious bulge in her pants. Katie noticed Lucy's expression and remembered the first time she'd been at Decadence, smiling in nostalgia. As Lucy's confidence had grown through the striptease course, she'd asked Katie if she could come with her to Decadance. Katie had been delighted. Maybe it would help Lucy get over Craig as much as it had helped her get over Stuart.

Then there was Sophie. When Katie had told her that Alex had suggested a night at Decadence, Sophie had looked sceptical – then said she'd come along with them for moral support. Even though Katie swore it was Alex's idea, Sophie was worried that he might feel out of his depth if he was the only non-fetishist in the club. When Lucy had expressed an interest in coming too her mind was made up. She had to come to look after everyone. She was a tad surprised by her consort, though.

After the debacle at the gallery, Sophie had run off to hide in the garden and cry. She couldn't believe she could go from feeling on top of the world to utterly humiliated in a matter of moments. When the celeb had followed her out to apologise for Celia's crass behaviour, she'd tried to hide her tears and told him it was no big deal, but he'd insisted on taking her out to dinner the next day to apologise.

Over dinner he'd told her that he'd dumped Celia for being so ungrateful: apparently her display at the gallery was the latest in a long line of embarrassing situations and he'd had enough. He and Sophie had spent the night chatting and laughing and when he'd suggested they meet up again, she'd instantly said yes. One meeting turned to another and now they saw each other every night that he was free, trying to make the most of every hour that he was in the UK. It seemed natural to Sophie to invite him to Decadance and, once he realised he could hide his identity behind a gimp mask, he said it sounded like 'a hoot'. Sophie swore to Katie that nothing had happened between them but Katie wasn't quite sure. And at the very least Sophie's career was on the up. The incident at the party had been written up in all the gossip mags and now she was a hot property, not least because half her paintings had been snapped up by the celeb's illustrious guests.

But really, the night was about Alex. Katie had been shocked when he'd mentioned going to Decadance together.

'You don't have to,' she said.

'Yes, but I want to. May as well see what all the fuss is about.'

Katie knew that he was making the effort for her but appreciated his offer.

'OK, but just to look. You don't have to feel obliged to play.'

❧

Four hours later, Ved and Amber were nowhere to be seen. Sophie had headed off to the dance floor with Lucy and 'the gimp', so Katie and Alex were left alone.

'So, what do you think?' she said.

'Seems harmless enough,' Alex said. 'OK, the fashion's a bit extreme.' He gestured at a man wearing nothing but a nappy. 'And I can't say the dungeon is my kind of place, but everyone seems nice.'

'Told you.'

'So, do you want to have a go on anything?'

'What?'

'You heard me. I know you said I don't have to play but it seems a bit mean bringing you here and not indulging. Do you want me to spank you or something?'

Katie thought about the idea of other people watching her being spanked by Alex but instead of her usual exhibitionistic thrill, she felt indignant.

'You know what? No. I don't want to share what we've got with anyone else. And as much fun as all that stuff is, it's not anything like as good as last night was.' Katie leaned over to Alex to kiss him, then pulled back abruptly as she realised what she'd said. 'Fuck, you've broken me.'

Alex smiled. 'Don't worry, honey, the feeling's mutual.'

'What do you mean?'

'Well, you might not want to be spanked by me here. But would it be a real turn-off if I put you over my knee when we get home? Ever since I saw that redhead in the corner writhing around getting spanked, I've had a hard-on thinking about having you in a similar position.'

Katie felt the blood rush to her clit.

'Are you turning kinky on me?'

'I don't know what you mean,' Alex said. 'Although you might want to check the bottom of the cupboard for a little present I got for you when we get home. Or should I say "box of tricks". I did learn a few things from Angela when I was with her, you know, and not all of them were bad…'

Katie gave Alex's cock a friendly squeeze and was gratified to find it engorged.

'OK, how about this. I'll let you spank me when we get back, and use your box of tricks, compelling as that sounds, on one condition.'

'Which is?'

'Afterwards, you fuck me. And I want you to look into my eyes as you come.'

Alex's kiss told Katie everything she needed to know.